An Imprint of HarperCollins*Publishers*

Digital Vampires

Nick leapt into the lift cabin and pushed the button marked CLOSE.

The doors rolled shut.

There was a thud on the door, and a muffled voice came from the other side, but it was too late. The lift began to move.

Suddenly, the cabin ground to a halt, and the trap door in the ceiling began to shift to one side.

Nick looked up.

Outlined against the beam of a floodlit shaft, hovering there silently like a huge praying mantis, was the angular outline of the Guardian. He was waiting.

The teeth cracked apart across the jaw into a dreadful grin.

Laurence Staig

Digital
Vampires

Lions
An Imprint of HarperCollins*Publishers*

ACKNOWLEDGEMENTS

Only a Northern Song and *All Together Now*
(John Lennon/Paul McCartney)
© 1968 Northern Songs, under licence to
SBK Songs Ltd, 3-5 Rathbone Place,
London W1P 1DA

First published in Great Britain
by HarperCollinsPublishers Ltd 1989
First published in Lions 1991

Lions is an imprint of
the Children's Division, part of
HarperCollinsPublishers Ltd,
77-85 Fulham Palace Road,
Hammersmith, London W6 8JB

ISBN 0 00 674268-8

Printed and bound in Great Britain by
HarperCollins Book Manufacturing, Glasgow

▶ CONTENTS

For Malcolm Saunders

In memory of the Duke de Richleau, Professor
Bernard Quatermass and the roof tops of South
London

"If you're listening to this song
You may think the chords are going wrong
But they're not; we just wrote them like that
When you're listening late at night
You may think the band are not quite right
But they are, they just play like that . . .
. . . If you think the harmony
Is a little dark and out of key
You're correct, there's nobody there."

ONLY A NORTHERN SONG
Lennon and McCartney

". . . Look at me
All together now, All together now . . ."

ALL TOGETHER NOW
Lennon and McCartney

". . . it's just technique, baby,
the way I do it, baby,
it's just technique."

TECHNIQUE
Jerry Lennox

"A previous time . . ."

He sat cross-legged within the perfect pattern of the pentacle – a young man, grey-faced with several days stubble on his chin. He looked weary, worn down by the months which he had spent trying to save his business from ruin. Now he must try his final option.

At last he was alone.

He would have to be quick. The others had been sent home hours ago. Only the Security Guards remained downstairs and they had strict instructions not to enter the penthouse suite without "the correct word".

He had from moonrise to dawn to complete the act. To find out if the "summoned one" would smile upon him and come to his aid in the name of the Dark Lord.

His restless eyes scanned the dome above. Through the central opening he watched the shimmering edge of the quarter crescent moon

11

as it floated gently into view.

Outside, a sudden breeze blew up.

It was late now. The hour was approaching.

The flames which lit the five points flickered. The candle at the northern point melted from a yellow to a bright blue flame, before being quickly extinguished, leaving a fine, curly trail of scented smoke. The candle to the west did the same, allowing a hungry moon to devour what light there was.

A deep smell of musk and damp earth filled the air.

From the outer edges of the room came a sound. It was like the slap of a wet mop. Something crept forward, a huddled thing. It seemed old, very old. The object slipped and slithered its way across the polished floor, heaving and squeezing towards the life-giving centre of the ring.

The creature had not been summoned since the awakening of the Grand Master, Jacques de Molay, all those centuries before. Who dared now to rouse the Dark Lord from the centuries of sleep, to command that it should rise from the labyrinth?

All that pain. The pain of returning. There had to be a price.

The resurrected one would not return without some prize.

"Baphomet," whispered the young man. "Baphomet. I am here to bargain, to trade."

The crawling ceased.

The shaggy loose flesh, fur, bone and hoof finally came together from out of the darkness.

Animal eyes, slit green, yet sharp as a blade, saw all.

From one corner of the pentacle a sacrificial white hen struggled to free itself from its ties.

In another corner a black cock had long given up the struggle.

"I am willing to exchange. To deal. What must I do?" asked the young man.

His pupils were bright.

"What I have is not enough. I want to know more, I want to taste more. I want more. You can give me wealth and good fortune."

A thick and guttural voice replied, a treacle mix of words which hung within poisoned sacs of air.

"There can be an arrangement." There was silence for a moment and then the voice continued. "But the price is high."

"Are you good enough to join?"

"It's like a mirror – but a mirror full of rainbows," said Suzie-Q, as she held the circular silver disc at a tilt, a little away from her.

The disc was almost magical, a drowning pool of images. Her own cherubic face, framed in square cut, blonde hair, darted into view momentarily.

Reflected fluorescent light fittings burned back from the edges. The rows of record albums, neatly stacked on metal shelving, and the bright advertising posters filled the surface with a haze of angled paint-box colour.

Above this jazz of images there floated a patch of ever-changing pastels, yellow and light blue bands which busily merged into one another. A further tilt of the disc and they would disappear, only to reappear on the opposite side. This time her own reflection peered back at her again, for a moment, before vanishing.

The air was filled with rock history. Shop owner, Dizzy Richards, was trying to sing along to his well worn copy of Jerry Lennox's famous song "Technique". Jerry Lennox: the greatest rock singer and guitarist to have come out of the '60s. *The* Master of lead guitar. Worshipped twenty-four hours a day in the little Battersea record shop.

The kids liked the song, they knew it by heart, but it wasn't a great help in their search for the "new" sound. It never seemed to leave the record deck. Dizzy just wasn't interested in current stuff. It was a miracle that compact discs had crept into his stock at all.

The record tried to interrupt Suzie-Q's thoughts, offended by her preoccupation with compact discs and digital technology.

An original gold disc copy of "Technique" sat proudly in an old Bakelite frame, beside '60s LP sleeves, which stared challengingly down from the walls above the racks. It was real gold, Dizzy had checked it out.

Beside the gold disc, within its own clip frame of glass, was pressed Jerry's obituary column from the *Melody Maker*. Dizzy had written it himself.

"Give it here," said Dizzy as his arm leant over from the record counter. "Silver crap. Anyone would think that you'd never seen one before. They may be tougher than vinyl but that doesn't mean that they're indestructible. These things are for playing, not for looking at your bloody self in. You've got to be careful with them." Then he added, "And they cost a packet."

"They're getting cheaper," smiled Suzie-Q. "I might just buy one to use as a fabby powder compact. What d'you think?"

"They just sound good," snapped Nick, who was busily poking his nose into the box which housed the latest CD releases. The spiked, jet black hair stuck out from the box like an obscure species of plant. "CDs are OK by me," he continued, "at least I don't have to move my arse any more to turn the record over, and I can programme tracks to play in any order I like."

"You know how they work, smart-pants?" asked Suzie-Q.

Nick shifted to one side, looking uncomfortable.

"Yeah, sort of. Digital is just another way of storing information. It's too complicated to explain to you lot but it's a good clean system. Great sounds and all captured in tiny pits of information in the disc, like grooves in a record."

"Shit thing," mumbled Dizzy as he lovingly took the 45 single off the old Garrard SP25 Mark II player. "Give me grooves. Grooves are groooovy, pits are . . . well . . . a pity."

He laughed at his own joke as he wiped the 45 clean with a felt cloth.

Suzie-Q groaned. Nick just shook his head.

Dizzy lifted the record reverently before the Bakelite frame like a priest with the sacrament.

"Here's to you, Jerry," he said as he replaced it back in its cardboard sleeve. "One day we'll spin the Goldie Oldie itself!"

"That thing will actually play, it's not just decoration?" asked Nick.

"'Course," clipped Dizzy. "Records are records. Just 'cos that one's gold and the others are black. The grooves are still there. Records have got an honest simplicity. Perhaps I'm an ancient but I stock and sell far more records than these compact things. Besides, LP sleeves are better. Bigger. You can get more information on them. Album design is an important art form, you know. All you get with these things is a little pull-out booklet in a cheap case."

"You sell more records because almost all your customers are retired hippies," snapped Nick.

Dizzy snorted.

"Hippies maybe, but they ain't retired."

Suzie-Q winked at Dizzy as she reluctantly returned the CD.

"You promised to get me a CD player for my next birthday, if I want," she cooed.

"I thought you kids were trying to get this band of yours together," said Dizzy a little sternly. "Perhaps you should have some proper musical instruments rather than all these push-button things. You lot make me laugh sometimes, a group with a name but no direction because you don't know where to go with your music. Play, sod it. Art and craft. Get on with it. I'll get you a proper instrument for your eighteenth, but I ain't getting you no CD player or push-button soulless computerized cow horn!"

Nick's pale face looked up.

"Keep him sweet, Suzie-Q. We need a micro-phone and you are supposed to be the singer. You had microphones in your day, Dizzy, re-member."

Dizzy placed the silver circle back into its sleeve.

"Cheeky little rat." His sense of humour re-turned. He couldn't be mad with them for long. "Anyhow, Miss Suzie-Q, you're independent now. Flown the nest. Own place. You want a CD, save up out of your grant, like I had to when I was a teen."

Suzie-Q dropped her head, slightly ashamed at having jogged him about the birthday. Dizzy had been good to her. Brought her up like she was his own.

His eyes glazed for a second. They often did, when softened with nostalgia.

"I remember my student days, we played our wax on the old SP25 and we used to stack our LPs up on planks, supported by bricks. We'd pick up old building bricks from the dumps in Moss Side at the back of the university near the Labour Club. These days it's all high-tech shelving. You get neat little moulded plastic things to put your neat little plastic cases into. There they are, ready to listen to with your neat little moulded minds!"

Nick rolled his eyes. Dizzy was going off again. His occasional trip back to the '50s was bad enough: juke boxes, DA haircuts and Buddy Holly. But the '60s hippies and joss sticks and peace and love could be so boring at times.

Then Nick saw the Dark Side CD.

He picked it out of the rack and held it close to his face, inches from his nose. He stared at it for several minutes in silence. Suzie-Q looked over. He was frozen like a statue. She watched him. It fascinated him, for some reason. It was unlike Nick to be so quiet.

"What have you got there?" she asked.

"I don't know," he said quietly. "It says something about a new breed of music for 'tomorrow's young musicians' – that's the bit that caught me, that's us, isn't it? We're tomorrow's musicians."

"Time will tell," sighed Dizzy as he turned round to count up the sales figures on his sheet, again. "As far as I'm concerned you're not even 'today's' yet. It depends on whether you're all going to chuck college in, like you keep threatening. If this band ever gets going, it'll be a miracle. If it were me then . . . "

"Let me look," interrupted Suzie-Q, snatching the case from his hand.

A crowd of faces stared back at her through the cover of the plastic frame. It was like a family portrait.

"I like the design, all those people. It's like that old Beatles record, 'Sergeant Pepper'. Not many sleeve notes, though. What's it say here?"

She mused over the blurb at the bottom of the cover, "Dark Side Discs. DigiWave, announcing the greatest band in the world, to be amongst you . . . very soon."

Suzie-Q wrinkled her nose at the paragraph beneath this.

19

"Are you good enough to join? Track 7 tells you how."

She threw Dizzy a quizzical look.

"Are you good enough, greatest band, track 7? What's all this then?"

"You've found that thing in there have you?" asked Dizzy as his head reappeared from behind the shop counter, "I've got a poster to put out as well. That's a weird one. It's a limited edition – big promotion. Distributed by that huge London megastore chain Merlin Records. It's a new label and a bargain they say, only £3. It's all a pile of junk, hype of course, a trailer for their new band. Manufactured, mass media, so on and so on. Only two thousand discs pressed. The series is supposed to be a sampler of 'the new sound'. This one's called DigiWave music. It's going to be a sensation, of course, so Merlin tells us dealers."

Nick looked up.

"Merlin? New sound. New?" This interested him.

"They even offered me a dumpbin and leaflets," continued Dizzy, "but that would be all too much for my little shop. I'd have had to take a minimum order too. It's difficult enough getting you lot to buy anything."

"Why did you order it at all?" asked Nick. "Doesn't sound like your sort of thing."

"No, it didn't grab me, but you know what I'm like, 'keep everybody happy', I try to keep a bit of everything. I am broader minded than you lot would like to think and the release sheet says that the disc is for 'tomorrow's musicians'.

That's the reason I got it, I suppose. The 'tomorrow's musicians' bit."

"We're almost there already," said Nick seriously. His gaze still rested on the CD cover.

Dizzy raised an eyebrow.

"There are supposed to be other big promotions too," he added, " If you play an instrument there's a way of getting a free ticket to the opening night of that new rock club, what's it called, the place they're all going on about, off Oxford Street?"

"Lasers," said Nick confidently. He knew it, of course. But then he would. Nick knew the London venues.

"That's it, Lasers," said Dizzy, "but I don't know how you claim the ticket, that track gives the answer, I suppose. It's an advertising stunt, a weird way of getting kids to part with their money and fill the new club on the first night! It's clever, typical of their style. Probably all down to Merlin's rich boss!"

"Lasers is supposed to be something else, though," said Suzie-Q. "It's due to open soon."

Dizzy thought for a moment.

"Wait a minute, I'll show you some of the gear they sent me if you're really that interested. There was tons of it, chucked most of the stuff out, though."

He disappeared again behind his counter of junk.

After a moment the gangly frame emerged with a large coloured poster. One hand searched for Blu-tack as the other tried to spread the sheet out on the wall beside the counter.

"Been meaning to put this up. Suppose I better do it now. It's only a replica of the sleeve, but I'll give it to them, it looks quite good. The Beatles did it first, of course. This outfit has just nicked the idea."

The two kids looked hard at the poster.

The picture showed a crowd of waving figures looking upwards towards the viewer. They were mostly young people, all shapes and sizes with different kinds of dress. They appeared to be a fairly normal crowd at first sight, and they were all smiling. Some held guitars, others waved drumsticks, or clamped elbows held keyboards neatly tucked under their arms, like daily newspapers. Nick didn't recognize anybody.

Suzie-Q thought that the picture might have been taken at an airfield, on a concrete runway, perhaps. There were white blocks and lines on either side of the assembly, like road markings, and there was nothing else for miles around. In an arc above the head of the group in red lettering was the title:

Dark Side Discs.

"Look at *him*," said Suzie-Q, pointing to a face in the corner of the poster. "He's creepy."

A large pointed hat sat above a craggy, white-bearded face. One eye was half closed, pulled downwards towards the cheek. The other eye was open – a gleaming watching orb.

"It says here: Merlin Records Ltd. A splendid time is guaranteed for all. Sample tomorrow today, sample DigiWave," said Nick. There was a tremor of excitement in his voice.

"Are you good enough to join us?" he continued reading. "What does that mean? Hey, perhaps we can tap into this new thing before it takes off!"

Suzie-Q wasn't quite convinced. Not quite. She felt uncomfortable and, besides, it was all too cosy. They were smiling just that little bit too much. Would the splendid time promised be that splendid?

Nick felt differently. A voice inside told him that he should buy it, and perhaps even try it.

"I'm good enough," he said seriously. "I can learn any new sound!"

Dizzy's shoulders heaved. "Mr Modesty! OK, you're not a bad keyboard player for a button-pusher but you don't want to take this too seriously."

Nick looked at the poster again, searching the faces in the crowd. Some of the kids in the picture had their palms turned inwards. Their saucer eyes were wide, really wide.

Suddenly a strange idea occurred to him, and it wouldn't go away.

"Are they waving?" he asked.

Suzie-Q looked over Nick's shoulder. "Yeah. Why d'you ask, what else could they be doing?"

"Beckoning," replied Nick.

"A crowd of people stood and stared . . ."

The kids' fascination with the poster was interrupted by a loud "clang", like a beaten dustbin lid.

Nick almost leapt from his skin.

The old shop bell had jangled its announcement of new customers. The kids hated the bell, left over from the time that Dizzy's shop had been a grocery store, but Dizzy refused to take it down. After all, it was old and, more importantly, it was original.

A black, leather-jacketed figure, with long arms and legs waving like an insect's, stalked into the shop.

It was Terry, the bass player. The personal stereo, as usual, was glued to his ears, holding his tightly frizzed hair in place like a metallic hair net. Close behind him strutted Josh, the drummer, appearing to shadow box his way in through the doorway (but without personal stereo). The familiar shades were wrapped round his face. A thin trail of dreadlocks tumbled out from beneath a top-heavy knitted beret.

Josh didn't need any headphone music.

His rhythm was natural. He was the best drummer around.

Now they were complete. All the members of Software House had arrived.

The band met in Dizzy's shop every Saturday lunchtime. It was habit by now, from the time that Suzie-Q had lived with Dizzy and Meg. Dizzy had encouraged them to use the place as a drop-in. He thought it would help the girl. Suzie-Q had always been a quiet kid. "A mixed up identity," had been one social worker's diagnosis, "and what about the peculiar Christian name?"

That had made Dizzy laugh. If only the guy had known.

Then recently she adopted this none too bright brother figure with the strange spiked hairdo, who kept failing his engineering exams at the tech. Things had got better lately. The day-dream band helped too.

The shop was never too busy, and being down a hidden Battersea back-street ensured its continued exclusivity. Only those that *knew* went there, usually collectors looking for rare records, or old mates of Dizzy's. Dizzy would suggest new titles for them to listen to. He even tried to help Software House put a repertoire together, lent them records for the weekend, but it was always old stuff. Nick had this thing about wanting to find a completely new sound.

Dizzy was a good mate, a bit out of place and strange with his pony tail and wire-rimmed granny spectacles, but a good mate all the same.

Terry and Josh were fun. Outrageous. But both were headstrong. Suzie-Q had lost count of the number of times she had talked them out of trouble. Terry usually greeted the others with an overblown demonstration of "long lost camaraderie", but today was different. The funny strut was there, but so too were serious expressions. Deadly serious.

Terry stopped in his tracks.

Dizzy was about to call out the usual, "Hi there, Spider Man," when he stopped himself.

There were bad vibrations today. He could tell, he had felt it the moment he had hauled himself out of bed. The planets were out of synch, he had felt it at morning meditation too. He hoped they weren't in trouble again.

Terry's face betrayed concern as soon as he had entered the shop. Even Josh had stopped shadow boxing to the music as he closed the door behind them, but he had also seen what had caught Terry's eye.

"Hey, Josh," called Terry, "come and cop this. There's even one here in Dizzy's shop, of all places. We'd better watch out."

The off button on the little white box, strapped to his belt, was clicked with a quick firm movement. The tinny beat stopped.

Terry looked at the newly displayed poster.

For a moment he said nothing. He walked directly up to the waving assembly and looked long and hard at the figures. A single finger traced the faces in the crowd. Slowly, he began to shake his head from side to side.

"See anyone you know?" joked Dizzy weakly.

"It's that Dark Side CD sampler."

Terry raised his voice slightly.

"You can only get this on compact disc. Did you know that, Dizzy, no black wax? So how come you've got it here, always thought that you were strictly a vinyl man?"

"Gotta keep up with the times," he replied.

"We've seen this before, haven't we, Josh? Up town, at the Merlin megastore. They were everywhere. So now you're stocking it here, eh?"

Terry's gaze remained on the poster, continuing his scan of the waving figures.

Dizzy wondered what was wrong. Terry's voice was disapproving.

"Have any of you heard this CD yet?" Terry continued. "It's a trailblazer for this mysterious new band."

"No, it's only just come in," said Dizzy, "and the CD player needs fixing. It's only a fuse. It didn't like being connected in with all my old gear. What were you doing in another record shop anyhow?"

"What's the matter, Tel?" asked Suzie-Q, with increasing interest.

She stopped flicking through the albums.

Terry ignored her question.

"Remember the ones we saw in Merlin, Josh?"

Josh sloped over, removed his dark glasses to a point an inch above his nose and scrutinized the sheet. Suzie-Q noticed a puffy bloodshot eye but said nothing.

"Relax, man, you're making too much of this, at least they ain't fighting."

Dizzy had now completely stopped working on his figures and was observing all of this with an interest which grew by the second.

"Fighting, fighting with who? Have you lot been in more trouble? Look, would one of you mind telling me what's going on?"

Josh placed his glasses back on the bridge of his nose.

"Tel and me we went into Merlin last week," he began. "You know, just to look around. We weren't cheating on you, honest. Stock's a bit bigger, though. This CD was in there. In fact it was all over the place. It was causing a real sensation, the centre of attention, you might say."

"There was trouble," said Terry, "funny trouble. It started at the enquiries desk."

"Three boys, right," Josh bounced back in. "The kids were being given a hard time by these store security guards. You know, they call them this poncy name – Megastore Guardians. Soften the image, all so cosy, but they're bully boys just the same. These boys were complaining about this CD, this one here. We think the kids were in a band and had bought copies. We didn't take a lot of notice at first, but then it got rough. Arguing and screaming. Something had happened to a couple of these guys, but we're not sure what. One kid got frog-marched off by two of these Guardians, but he wasn't taken to any office."

28

Josh lowered his voice.

"Tel and me followed. The kids were younger than us and those so called 'Guardians' were *heavy*. They didn't see us at first. One kid got taken to this side corridor near one of the exits." He paused as he looked towards Terry. "We think they only managed to break his nose and cut him up a bit."

"Broke his nose! Cut him up a bit!" yelled Dizzy angrily. "They beat the kid up? Why? Are you sure they weren't messing around, some mistake or something? Was it reported?"

Josh shook his head.

"No, this was serious shit, like he'd committed a bad crime. The kid hadn't done anything wrong and it was two to one. The other little guy ran off somewhere, so . . . "

There was a pause.

"We helped out a little," said Terry.

"Helped out?" asked Suzie-Q, as she raised her eyes to the ceiling. Trouble! Again.

"Those guards were animals, they didn't even seem like a regular security mob, they were sort of, well, funny. The kid was yelling about how they'd nearly lost their friend because of the CD, what were Merlin up to, and so on."

"What was it one of the others said?" Terry tried to remember. "That oddball thing, couldn't have him or something? Yeah, that was it: *They couldn't have him.* Man, was he making a fuss!"

"Couldn't have him?" repeated Suzie-Q.

"Is that it?" asked Dizzy.

Terry and Josh looked at one another.

"Ain't that enough? You weren't there, man,"

said Josh firmly. "Those guards went berserk. One of them, a heavy guy, with this peaked cap and weird face, told them to keep their mouths shut if they knew what was good for them, I got an eyeful and Terry nearly got his arm wrenched off. They said it was none of our business. I grabbed the kid outside before he ran off, asked him what was up. He was in tears, didn't want to talk at first, didn't even thank us for helping out like. He said he was too scared to say much. Then he did say a crazy thing. It kinda slipped out."

Josh shifted from one foot to another. He swallowed.

"He looked straight at us. The kid was in another world. He said that he couldn't play the guitar now, couldn't do anything any more, his mate couldn't even tap out a simple drum rhythm on a drum pad, and it was all the fault of this disc, some special track? Anyhow, this was the second time they'd come back. He said that Merlin could keep their free tickets, they didn't have to go, did they? He grabbed me by the shirt as he said it. It was a kinda frightened question. He staggered off before we could get any more."

Josh looked directly at Terry.

"It was the way he looked," whispered Terry. "His eyes. They were all empty, frightened. He was scared, man, and it frightened the hell out of me too. Guardians!"

Nobody said a word. Despite the bright sunshine, the day took on a greyer shift.

"Stop it, you lot. You're giving me the creeps," said Suzie-Q.

Terry and Josh remained stone-faced.

Dizzy thought hard. He was upset. Was it worth storming up there, phoning? Probably not. He hated violence of any kind. Especially from people in uniform. Megastores, bovver-booted guards with fancy names. Compact discs! They should have stuck with their local shop and honest black wax. The hard sincerity of the story worried him. Josh and Terry were rough diamonds but never told lies, and he'd never seen them bothered like this before.

Nick had gone unusually quiet. He had been looking into the poster.

"I want a copy," he said suddenly. "I want to hear it at home."

His face shone.

"Nick?" said Suzie-Q slowly. She shook his arm. He seemed far away.

"I'm good enough." He continued, "Really I am."

Dizzy was startled.

Thinking quickly, he grabbed the disc from the counter.

"Oh no. I'm not having you waste your money. In any case, this is going back where it came from. The Merlin Megawhatever can go stuff themselves."

He glanced up at the Jerry Lennox golden disc.

"Digital bollocks! Give me that man any day. He knew how to sing, and play? Man, there were nights when we were on the road together when he could make time stand still, a trickle of notes that seemed so easy and yet

31

were so hard. Rumour was he taught Clapton too. The day that Jerry Lennox's plane went down was the day part of pop history died."

Suzie-Q shivered.

Dizzy tried to make a joke. It had got too serious.

"Keep with the black stuff and I promise not to rough any of you up." He attempted a smile.

Nick remained in front of the poster.

"Well," asked Suzie-Q, breaking the long pause, "after all of this, just what is the name of this *wonderful* new band that we're supposed to look out for?"

"They ain't saying yet," said Josh. "But there were big window displays at Merlin. Whoever they are, they're going to play live at the opening night of that new club. There was this flame effect thing with laser lights in the store."

Dizzy's face showed concern. Today's scene worried him. The actual violence of it, real violence sometimes, and that anger, all that energetic waste. Rock music had had its casualties in his day. There had been great talent that couldn't slow down and move out of the so-called fast lane. Now there were other motorways bringing with them new waves of technology. Automatic music and something called DigiWave? Store guards beating up customers!

But there was more. He had a nose for trouble.

He looked up at the poster again, and then down at the CD.

The members of Software House stood still,

staring at the poster, frozen within the moment.

"Dark Side Discs . . ." said Nick.

Merely mentioning the name now brought an icy feeling to the meeting.

All the fun had gone out of their Saturday.

Dizzy tilted the silver disc. Its black shadow stretched out into a long oval, almost covering the counter top.

The old shop bell released a sudden single muffled note, it broke the silence. All eyes turned to the door but it remained closed.

Nobody had entered or left.

There was a sudden crack as though a heel had trodden on something.

Suzie-Q jumped.

The CD, which Dizzy held in his hand, split into a forked jag like a cracked mirror.

Nick was still staring at the people in the poster.

The people in the poster stared back.

"Yeah, that's the word: contagious..."

"You will be careful, won't you?"

Suzie-Q's only girlfriend, Debbie, pulled an agonized expression as she fumbled around at the back of the television. Although she had managed to disconnect the set, the right plug for the new music centre didn't seem to want to know. Why were electrical sockets always in such hard to get to places?

"You'll have to be quick," she whined on. "This gear's Dad's pride and joy. None of us is allowed to even so much as breathe on it. If he comes home and finds that I've been letting you mess about ..."

"Debbie," said Suzie-Q firmly. "Please don't go on. I only want to play one track on it. One track! Dizzy doesn't know I've got the disc so I've got to smuggle it back into the shop Monday morning."

"Shouldn't be too difficult," said Debbie,

straining her neck round the back of the television trolley. "I know he was sort of your foster dad and everything, but that bloke's usually in another dimension. 'Heh, maaan, outa sight, tooo much, heh, listen to this.' Is he still into all that green magic stuff, sitting cross-legged on the floor and wholemeal bread and astrology. . . ? I thought him and Meg were moving to Cornwall soon. Got it!" She interrupted her impression as the plug was finally pushed home into its rather too snug fit.

"Dizzy's OK," said Suzie-Q quietly.

Debbie bit her lip, she was on dangerous territory taking the rise out of Dizzy Richards.

"Sorry. Look, I didn't mean it. No harm meant. OK?"

Suzie-Q nodded. She was used to it.

"Now look. Do please be careful. All that this thing has had on it since Mum bought it for him has been Beethoven, Wagner and Loudon Wainright III and the Homesteaders. What is it you want to listen to, anyhow? They've only gone up to the Lord Stanley, you know."

Suzie-Q clicked open her shoulder bag.

The crowd looked up from the bottom of the bag, from out of the picture frame plastic case.

"I don't know really. It's supposed to be a new sound – something called DigiWave. Look, it's a bit of a story."

"Well, save it, but if it's rock music we'd better be careful. I'm not sure our CD player will stand the shock. We don't want to excite the poor thing. Give it here."

Suzie-Q took the plastic case out of her bag and snapped open the front cover. The silver sparkle had gone. Instead there were fleeting shapes that twisted like moonlit shadows.

She paused for a moment, but then sniffed away her fears and handed the CD to Debbie.

"We may get free tickets to the opening night of that new rock club," she added with a half-hearted grin.

Debbie turned back.

"Hey, you don't say? By listening to a compact disc?"

"It's a publicity thing. That's why I wanted to hear it. The instructions on how to get the tickets are on the disc itself."

Debbie frowned and shrugged her shoulders, not quite understanding.

Then she pressed a button.

Beside the television a short squat block of blackness suddenly flickered into life: an assortment of red and amber LED lights. The music centre glowed behind the security of an anonymous tinted grey glass door. An altar of high-tech. Debbie pressed opened the glass front and punched a switch on the compact disc player.

The whirr of a smoothly geared CD tray offered its tongue to receive. Debbie carefully laid the disc into the tray and waited for it to be taken into the body of the player.

"Quick now, all right, or Dad will kill me. Which track is it?"

"Seven," said Suzie-Q.

Debbie screwed her face up. There were

so many buttons. So many technical names: Store, Memory, Time, Select, Repeat, Error.

"I think it's this one." Debbie pressed a seven.

One stubbornly flashed up on the yellow digital display.

"Ohhh damn it!" She squeezed her hands into fists. "It won't do as it's told. I did tell you that it only likes classical rubbish."

She pressed seven again. The single slanted number one remained.

For a moment there was a black velvety silence. No hiss, no crackle. No pop. Just pure digitized silence.

After a few seconds the rough growl of a "game show" type voice cut across the tiny sitting room.

Both girls gulped. It had come as a shock, an intrusion.

Suddenly the sound was all around them.

"Hi. Please bear with us before you make your track selection. We have a message for you. The Merlin Records Corporation welcome you to our trailer for the best band in the world. Coming soon! A truly new sound awaits you: DigiWave. We want the newest neatest talent to join us at our opening night launch at *the* place to be – Lasers, so if you're a rising star, simply grab your instrument and find track seven at the end of this disc. Meantime here's half a dozen neat treats, a taste of DigiWave. But remember, this is *only* a taste!"

Suzie-Q reached out and held Debbie's arm.

It crept up on them at first.

Rubber band sounds cut into the evening.

And then, it was there with a startling immediacy.

The music rippled over them, through them. It squeezed its way under their skin. It was unlike anything they had ever heard before. A trickle of high-end notes tinkled the glasses out on the sink drainer. A bass pounded the walls.

"Wait a minute," said Debbie. "This is incredible. What is it? I've never heard anything like it!"

Suzie-Q felt strange.

"Let's turn it off. It's the wrong disc," she said.

Debbie turned on her. "No, leave it. It's sort of like folk music with all that electronic echo. It's crazy!"

Suzie-Q ran her fingers through her hair. There was something there from long ago, primitive, melted into the twentieth century with strange electronics. Beneath all that digitized wall of noise was another, very different kind of music.

Suzie-Q had had enough. "Dark Side" was a very good name for the series. She could listen to no more. The sound became hard like a drill which burrowed mercilessly into her head. She rushed past Debbie, over to the black block and turned controls on the amplifier section, desperately searching for the volume. A large round black knob lowered the blast.

But Debbie was captivated. She wanted it to go on for ever.

"Suzie-Q!" cried Debbie, as if suddenly

38

flipped back from somewhere else. "This is great, it's really getting me going, can't say much for the melody line, but it's addictive, kind of contagious, I suppose. Yeah, that's the word, contagious. Where'd you say you got it from? Dizzy's?"

"No, never mind. Switch it off. Your parents will be back."

"Don't worry about them," replied Debbie as she strutted over to the player. "Let's hear this other track, number seven. Free tickets too. This sounds too good to be true."

Suzie-Q had lost control.

Debbie repressed the button which belonged to seven, and increased the volume again.

The final harmonic of a guitar chord snapped abruptly into oblivion.

There was a silence once more, then the same "Game Show" voice they had heard a moment earlier returned.

"The Merlin Records Corporation wants you to enjoy good sounds whilst learning the newest sweetest hottest licks around, all on your own chosen instrument. Hope you've got it there with you now. You'll be taught by those from the shadows."

"It's a tutorial," said Debbie, "I haven't got a guitar or any . . . "

The commentary continued.

"This special opportunity is offered on this exclusive track and is available to every serious young musician. We will explain how in just a few moments. But first we want you to be relaxed and serious about your special audition. This is a precision disc, computed to allow you to show us what you can do. For this purpose you need to be alone when you listen to the rest of this track. We want your attention. We *need* your attention. Exclusively, OK? The disc can only attune to one musician at a time. One moment now whilst we run a check and you can prepare yourself."

Suzie-Q's eyebrows knitted into a frown.

"Run a check?" asked Debbie. "What's he talking about, what is this?"

The two girls looked at one another.

"I really think . . . " began Suzie-Q.

A fairy bell tinkle crept out from somewhere within the player. Then a click.

After a few moments the voice returned, but this time there was a cold edge to the announcement.

"Sorry, folks! We have computed that there are more than the permitted limit of listeners in the room. I'm afraid the Special Offer part of this disc cannot proceed at present. Pity. In the meanwhile please enjoy a selection of top cuts played exclusively for you by the Dark Side Disc Band. We are returning you to track one. Remember, if you want an exclusive invite to the premier rock club Lasers, to be there on that special night with other rising star musicians, do as we tell you."

The amber numeral 'one' flickered onto the player.

A synthesized rhythm bounced back into the room.

But Suzie-Q wasn't listening. The sinister edge of the last sentence rang within her head still. There had been something very unfriendly about the way it had said:

"Do as we tell you."

► TRACK 4

"... it's not my job to ask questions. They don't like that here..."

Nick had watched the Guardian for some while now. The figure hadn't moved. From the corner of the store a smile of white teeth gleamed beneath the sightless patches of drop-hood shades. A strange thick scar ran from a place beneath the peak of his cap down on to his nose. It practically divided the face into two.

Nick had been fascinated by the figure. It was unreal. The flesh was too waxen, a smooth polished beige, almost translucent. The huge folded arms reinforced the impression of someone who might be a jailer rather than a man simply responsible for the Oxford Street branch of Merlin Records, and only the rock music section of the compact discs at that!

All around them the cacophony of a usual busy London West End store thundered on. Loud rock was punctuated by announcements of special offers one would be crazy to miss.

Lighting effects threw waves of flame up on to the walls and ceilings whilst an occasional spatter of perfectly honed laser beam cut across the heads of the crowd of eager customers.

Nick had stood at the entrance to the store for a while, pondering over whether or not to head for the CD section where the Guardian stood.

A flashing, fizzing, red neon sign formed an archway above his head. The fabulous millionaire boss's welcome to his empire of everything for the discerning rock-popophile: CDs, T-shirts, books, records, posters, videos.

LE MARA'S MERLIN MEGASTORE, it said.

Nick had felt nervous about entering the building. There was of course an inner guilt about not getting the CD from Dizzy's shop. He needed the business, but what could he do? Dizzy, for some reason, wouldn't let him have one.

Nick's curiosity had grown by the hour.

He took a deep breath, entered and scanned the dumpbins that formed patterns of lonely islands around the shop floor.

Finding the Dark Side disc was proving more difficult than he had imagined. Terry and Josh had said that there were dozens of them packed into dumpbins and display trays, but now there was no sign of any copies at all.

Nick decided to ask.

"That was a special offer last week," said a blue-lipsticked, pale-faced store assistant. "That CD's been pulled now. I don't even know whether we've got one left in the stockroom."

Nick looked past her, busily searching the shelves and display units for the familiar crowd scene cover.

"But why? I mean, I thought it had only just been released? There were loads of them here last week, some mates of mine came in and got a couple."

"That was last week. They've all gone. I ain't lying. We've been told to withdraw the rest of the public stock. It all seemed a bit odd to me too, but then this is an odd place to work."

She lowered her voice. "It would be, being Simon Le Mara's set-up. Stingy cow. It's slave labour out here while he sits upstairs at designer desks, counting his money!"

The girl's blue lips pouted. "Do you like me? I only work here part-time, I sing in a band you know, gonna be famous one day. My name's Tracy."

Nick was thrown for a moment.

"Part-time?" he asked.

"Yeah. A month or two on and then you get the push. They're taking people all the time, it's policy. So's you don't get your feet too comfortably under the table. That's what I think anyhow. Why, are you looking for a job? Pays the rent. Suits me for now."

"Look, listen to me. The Dark Side CD, one copy perhaps?"

The assistant pouted her lips again and continued to put out the albums.

"So you don't fancy me, then?"

"But you must have some somewhere?" persisted Nick. He was becoming agitated. There were two different threads to the conversation and both operating simultaneously.

The waxen-faced Guardian from the corner of the CD section turned his fixed smile in Nick's direction. He had heard the anguished discussion and it had now gone on for too long.

The arms unfolded.

"Like I said, I only work here," said the assistant. "We're out of stock and the re-order sheets kept coming back marked up. Something like – *Enough Taken* is the usual message."

"Enough taken?" asked Nick.

"Search me. I don't understand it either, but then it's not my job to ask questions. They don't like that here. Questions are definitely a 'no-no' at Merlin. Look here, not supposed to do this but have a gander at my list, if you like. You're fabby, do you know that?"

A smirk crept on to Nick's face, but he was more interested in the sheet.

The assistant made a clucking noise with her tongue and flipped a page over the clipboard. Nick saw a red typed entry next to her blue-painted finger:

"*Enough taken stop promotion*," she read. "There you are."

The girl was about to return to her task of putting out new releases in the browser racks when an about turn brought her face to face with the Guardian. He had swiftly and silently glided over. His large hand caught the edge of her clipboard and firmly turned it down towards her side. The tiny reflection of her slightly-built frame burned back out of the darkness of the

45

drop-shade glasses. Her throat jerked with an uncomfortable gulp.

"Everything all right?" he asked coldly.

Nick backed away, the hairs on the nape of his neck bristled.

"The . . . the Dark Side CD," he stammered. "You had it here last week, on display. I wanted a copy of it, that was all. The ticket offer to Lasers."

For a moment the grin of teeth vanished. The polished face looked Nick up and down. The shades lifted for a second as the Guardian nodded at something or someone across the shop floor. Nick turned round to see who he could have been nodding at, but then, quite suddenly, a hollow empty laugh tumbled out from a place within the blue uniform.

"OK, Tracy, I'll handle this," said the Guardian.

An over-heavy hand slapped Nick on the back as the face lowered to his. Then he whispered in his ear, it seemed without breath.

"Are you sure now? Are you good enough? Do you know what I mean? Are you a really good musician? Mr Le Mara only wants really good musicians."

Nick was surprised to find himself smiling in return. He felt bathed in a warm comforting waft of air. Perhaps it was the air conditioning.

"Sure," he replied. "I'm good enough."

"Wait here, boy," said the Guardian. "Perhaps I can find one more copy . . . Just for you."

The Guardian turned towards a door marked Private.

The assistant had gone white.

"They're coming, you know," she said, abruptly changing the subject. "The best band in the world. There's a window display going up now."

Nick looked over her shoulder. Several other young Merlin store assistants were assembling man-sized letters in the front window. The display already gave part of the message:

Coming soon: DigiWave from Dark Side Discs. Live at Lasers:

T H E   I N

Another two girls were each struggling with a large letter: a *B* and an *I*.

Someone called out suddenly from within the shop window:

"Where's the bloody *U*?"

Then, from out of nowhere, the Guardian was back with a copy of the CD for Nick. It looked different though, he wasn't sure quite how, but it did.

"Here you are, a few senior staff can give a couple more out to special people. You're *very* special now, aren't you? I've also put a ticket for a certain opening night inside the case. Keep all this to yourself or everyone will want one."

The Guardian pressed the case into Nick's hand and then closed his fingers around the fist. He tapped the end of his nose. The hand was cold, icy cold, with a hard grip. The grip tightened, squeezing the sharp edges of the plastic into Nick's palm.

It hurt.

Nick winced.

The smile on the face of the Guardian returned.

"... all together now ... alltogethernow ..."

The room had been darkened.

The desk lamp which Nick usually shone down on to his turntable was now turned upwards, casting a widening ray of light across the wall. A moth fluttered and teased the opening of the shade, throwing ever-changing shadows within the wake of the beam.

Nick cracked his knuckles. He sat before the keyboard of his Yamaha X5000. Waiting and wondering.

It was like a dare, a dare with himself. With the parents out for the evening and the band meeting cancelled, the moment was opportune.

Nick had to try it out for himself. Already having a ticket for Lasers wasn't enough. He needed to listen to the track, to discover what it was about. He had to know.

He had already heard the introductory section through his headphones, but had not bothered to listen to the sampler tracks of DigiWave. He was too impatient, he wanted to audition. The Yamaha had been at home for the weekend so it was now a simple matter of opening up the case, setting up and switching on.

At last he was ready for the track that held the secrets: would he be good enough to join?

With the exact reverence of a special ceremony he removed his headphones and switched the CD player over to audio.

His left hand reached for the infra-red remote control for his Mission 7000, a single squeeze aimed in the direction of the CD player started the disc. A tinkle, like a far off wind chime, announced that the disc was being read.

The table lamp suddenly dimmed, as though there had been a mains dip. The CD player's LED lamps glowed. A voice cut through the gloom.

Nick's fists tightened in anticipation.

"The Merlin Record Corporation want you to enjoy good sounds whilst learning the newest sweetest hottest licks around, all on your own chosen instrument. Hope you've got it there with you now. You'll be taught by *our* tutors. This special opportunity is offered on this exclusive track and is available to every serious young musician. We will explain how in a few moments but first we want you to be relaxed about your special audition. This is a precision disc, computed to allow you to show us precisely what you can do. For this purpose you need to be alone when you listen to the rest of this track. We want your attention. We NEED your attention. Exclusively. OK? One moment now whilst we check the scene and you can prepare yourself."

The silence returned. The CD tinkled once more.

"Hi, there. Well, that's better. That shop was stuffy, wasn't it?"

Nick blinked.

"Let's see what you can do then. A simple 12-bar boogie coming up, get into the beat and let your fingers trickle out those notes . . . play along with DigiWave. Have fun! Be happy! But first we need to connect! Now here's how we do it. If your instrument has a standard phono fitting on the end of its lead then simply plug straight into auxiliary at the back of your amplifier. That way we can monitor you. If not, then don't worry, place your instrument's speaker as close to the CD tray as you can. We'll pause to let you sort that one out. Catch you in a moment!"

Nick couldn't believe what he was hearing. Without thinking he reached for the bureau drawer and quickly found a phono lead. Within seconds he had connected the output of the Yamaha to the rear of the hi-fi amplifier.

"OK, rightee-oh let's go," said the voice on the CD.

The crisp snap of a Hi-Hat cracked out in

front of him, followed by a guitar intro that begged for a bass run from the lower octave of the Yamaha. Nick was swept up with the beat. His fingers raced across the keys, filling in with complex runs and trills that he had never even dreamt he could handle. His own potential grew before his eyes, his playing was getting better and better. The fourth dimension of sound had opened out there and then in the living room of 14 Palace Road.

They were rolling, they were getting there.

The rhythm captured his soul, his hands becoming an extension of the keys.

A voice from the CD said, "YEAH!"

Nick replied, "You've got it!"

"Stroll on!" cried the voice.

The shadow of the moth grew, the kaleidoscope of shapes bounced and flickered with the beat. The outline became harder, blacker, somehow less like an insect's. It was more like the sharp angular kite shape of bat's wings.

The CD player shuddered with the music.

The voiceover suddenly cut in.

"Hey, yeah, that's real neat, you sure can cut it. OK, my man, let's give it some beef, eh? Let's give it *power*. See what you can really do."

Nick took the lead riff and turned up the volume on the Yamaha.

His hands lifted into the air for a few moments, large hovering spiders which lunged suddenly into the river of ebony and ivory. His fingertips

caressed the keys, the keys caressed his fingertips.

"My maan," came the voiceover. "You're
cool, do you want to join the band, the Best
Band in the World, do you?"

Nick continued playing.
He tried to speak, but the excitement knotted
his tongue. He stuttered a staccato series of
"yes ... yes ... yes ... " It was a crazy
tutorial method but the drive and the music
were fantastic.
The voice returned, loud and clear.

"I SAID – DO YOU WANT TO JOIN THE
BEST BAND IN THE WORLD – LET ME HEAR
YOU SAY YEAH!"

Nick laughed. It was talking to him personally.

"LET ME HEAR YOU, BOY – LET ME
HEAR YOU. ARE YOU GOING TO PLAY
ALONG OR JOIN? WE WANT YOU, ARE
YOU GOOD ENOUGH? GOOD ENOUGH FOR
THE NEW SOUND, THE DARK SOUND, LET
ME HEAR YOU SAY ... "

"YEAH!" cried Nick, "I'm good enough.
YEAH! YEAH! YEAHHHH!"

"Right on!" came the reply, "Call Merlin
Megastore, quote code 1999 for your ticket to

Wonderland. Remember that: 1999. OK. Let's go. Let's have some. Like the fab four used to say – ALL TOGETHER NOW, alltogethernow!"

The CD engaged overdrive, turbo drive, ultimate drive.

The voiceover became louder, repeating the same phrase over and over and over again.

"Alltogethernow, alltogethernow, alltogethernow!"

Faster and faster. Faster and faster.

"Alltogethernow, alltogethernow."

A kite-shaped shadow reared up from the edge of the room.

The rainbow secrets of the silver disc spilled out from the disc drawer. They rushed and swept paths of silver light around him, like miniature shooting stars.

Somewhere in the background a chanting started up, mingling with the rise and fall of the melody line. It was an older sound and it was trying to break through. A choir, and singing in a *foreign* language? He couldn't tell, but he didn't care.

The CD drawer opened like the well-greased drawbridge of a magic castle, a powerhouse of laser light.

The occupants floated out.

Small shining orbs of multi-coloured rays floated up and away from the tray, like soap bubbles. There were only a few small orbs at first, but then, as the tempo of the music increased, so did their size. It was as if the disc inside the player had inflated from its usual flat silver platter and was softly blowing bubbles out into the room.

A rolling flow of reds, yellows and blues passed in front of his keyboard.

There was movement.

There was something inside each orb.

Nick's jaw slackened, he stopped playing, his hands froze above the keys.

He felt the edge of fear.

Behind each rainbow bubble screen a figure twisted and turned. A bubble larger than the others passed by. Inside he could just make out a kid about his own age. He was furiously thrashing for all his worth at a drum set. Other bubbles followed, all containing young musicians with guitars, keyboards or other instruments. But there were other figures too, and they looked less human.

Nick pushed the keyboard away. He looked about him, anxiously searching for the door. He'd forgotten where it was and where HE was. An empty bubble which had been drifting to the rear of the room approached him from the back. The soft skin of the orb gently kissed his body. The yielding soapy-like film wrapped itself around him.

He became limp. His anxiety left him.

The thrill of the tempo returned, racing through his veins and burning him up like a hungry furnace. A smaller orb floated past at eye level. Through a shadowy veil within the orb, Nick saw something small and black which crouched at the centre. Two specks, like red hot coals, burned back at him. Behind the figure were neatly folded tucks of smooth black velvet, like wings.

"With me, with me," said a voice.

A vast and empty hollow opened out beneath the red eyes. It took him in. All of him. Sucking at his vitality, draining it out of him like thick cream through a straw. There was a soft, pleasant, yielding sensation.

It comforted.

He wanted to go, to let all of it go.

He felt turned inside out.

The last thing he remembered was the break-up. Everything around him fitting into compartments, sets of neat and tidy blocks.

He had been taken. In sections.

He felt part of a great digital picture.

When Suzie-Q entered the living room she found Nick lying at a very awkward angle in front of the sofa. She peered down at him and then shook him hard. His eyes flicked open. At first he didn't recognize the round face and blonde hair.

"1999! 1999! 1999!" he screamed.

"Nick! Nick! It's me, Suze. What's been going on? The front door was open! Nick!"

"Ticket ... ticket ... want to join ... no ... no ... 1999 ... "

"What is it, what's the matter?" she cried, as she shook him again.

Nick didn't answer. He had a wild look about him and continued to cry out.

Suzie-Q slapped him on the face. He suddenly stopped shouting.

He felt cold and peculiar inside.

The living-room light had now been switched on. The spaghetti tangle of cables and leads from the Yamaha lay strewn around his feet.

He tried to get up, but fell limply back against the sofa again.

"A dream . . . was it a dream? Ticket number 1999. They can't make me join . . . can they?" he mumbled.

"Of course not. No. Wait a minute," said Suzie-Q, "I'm going to get you some tea. I don't know what's been going on here. Look at the place."

She swiftly disappeared through the door and out into the kitchen. Nick peered wearily across at his CD deck. He couldn't remember anything clearly. Only flashes, without a proper sequence.

The CD drawer was open.

Staggering to his feet, he stretched out his hand towards the player and lifted the silver disc from the drawer.

It felt wet, slimy, as if snails had crawled all over it.

A single small silver bubble on the fireside rug shimmered for a few seconds before finally bursting.

A small, black, wet stain remained on the rug.

He struggled to remember.

Eyes. Silver rays and a creature. There was a creature.

There had been something black and unpleasant.

Suzie-Q stood in the doorway holding the CD case. It had been lying on the kitchen table.

"You played it?" she asked.

He nodded.

"Did you play track seven?"

His face held the answer, but he couldn't explain anything to her. He felt all used up, like a wrung-out rag. He took a step forward and then fell awkwardly down on to the rug in a dead faint.

Suzie-Q cried out and dropped the case.

"... he was a nutter, lived on his own in a round room ..."

"It's just technique, baby,
  The way I do it, baby,
  It's just technique!

My rhythm's natural, sugar,
  Not artificial, sugar,
  It's just technique!"

Jerry Lennox rocked out of the front door of the little record shop in Harbour Avenue as usual.

"Here it comes now, the guitar break!" screamed Dizzy as he yanked the broom handle up into a mock guitar. It was back to the old days, playing again, just like the time he stopped being a roadie and played on stage with Jerry that night at Crawdaddy's. It was a double bill with the Yardbirds, before they got big.

59

He bent an E sharp with his middle finger and got a splinter.

Dizzy was in early that morning. Meg had been away for two months now and he'd got used to it. In any case, he liked to sweep up, a general tidy round before his one or two faithful regulars would storm the shop for the usual chat and mug of coffee, decaffeinated of course.

The days passed in reminiscence and debate: if Big Nigel of Greenwich came over, there would probably be an argument over who was the father of rock and roll and whether or not The Beat of Soweto had been influenced by the music of the 1950s. There might even be some speculation about what would have happened to Buddy Holly if he had lived. Recently there had even been serious talk over whether or not the Beatles would have reformed had John Lennon not been shot in a New York street. And where would any of them have been anyway if there hadn't been the musical influence of Jerry Lennox?

If Judy was down from the north, Dizzy might be asked to prepare a personal horoscope, for someone she knew, or even a biorhythm chart for herself. He might be asked to take the odd martial arts class, maybe for some of Nick's engineering student friends.

Who knows? Life was busy.

He might even sell some records, but it didn't really matter.

The Yuppies were coming, they were even pushing out the Muesli belt now.

The lure of Battersea Village, as it was now

known, was growing. He had only to hold out a little longer before he would be selling the shop and its desirable but at present run-down flat above to a Double Income No Kids set. Then he and Meg could retire to Cornwall and set up a no hassle business in the "fruits of the earth" without her having to drag around in the van every other month selling on the road. Maybe they could even take on a bit of organic farming. It would be easier now that the kid was up and living away from home. He'd kept his promise to the man. She'd grown up as their own.

Bert Radcliffe's old grocery shop was fast becoming a gold mine.

It would probably end up as an antiques emporium.

He'd miss the kids, though. They were great. If only they could understand what he was talking about sometimes.

Values, though! Where were the values?

He sounded like his own father.

A final quick sweep of the brush over the pavement to the gutter and he had finished. He leant his broom against the shop window and carefully removed the gold weave headband from round his head.

He adjusted his wire-rimmed spectacles and gazed down the road towards the junction. The noise of the busy Battersea traffic two blocks further up announced the beginning of a new day. A heat haze was already beginning to mist the distant view of the railway goods yard.

Then he saw two familiar figures turn the corner of Jinks Road.

Dizzy sniffed, and checked his wristwatch. He was sure it was Nick and Suzie-Q, but this was not the time they usually visited. For a start, it was far too early. He waved whilst picking up his broom. The kids stopped for a moment. He was not sure whether or not they had seen him. They were talking, engrossed, so he thought.

This was most unusual.

He continued to watch. After a moment they moved on, now hurriedly advancing up the street towards the shop. There seemed to be something wrong with Nick, he was having difficulty walking properly. A few minutes later and they were upon him. Nick's face looked drawn, as though he hadn't slept for weeks.

"Dizzy, you're here," said Suzie-Q, "we hoped you would be. We've gotta talk to you!" She ran ahead of Nick and grabbed Dizzy roughly by the arm. Not even a morning peck on the cheek.

"Can we go inside?" she asked.

"Sure," said Dizzy. "What's the problem? Nick looks terrible!"

Suzie-Q pulled Dizzy into the shop. Nick stumbled behind.

The old grocery bell clunked its confirmation of a tightly shut front door. Jerry Lennox had finished on the turntable, the stylus was grating inwards and outwards from the record label, impatiently asking to be lifted off the record and replaced in its rest. The auto-changer still needed fixing.

"Let me put this Golden Oldie away, and I'll put the radio on for a bit of background. One good thing about compact discs, I suppose, is that you don't have to keep messing around with tone arms!"

At the mention of compact discs the two kids looked at one another. Nick coughed and looked down at the floor.

Dizzy reverently lifted the record into the air before the hallowed golden disc that looked down from the wall. This was the usual ritual. Reverence to the King of the '60s sound.

Suzie-Q dragged out two old paint-spattered chairs from behind Dizzy's counter and offered one to Nick. Dizzy had returned to the back of the shop for a moment. Suzie-Q lifted a single finger to her lips and shook Nick by the shoulder. He looked up and nodded. He was still feeling drowsy. They were to keep quiet about things for now.

"What can I do for you?" called Dizzy from the back room, "or is this just a drop in? It's rather early for a debate on pop culture and why we're all here."

"You know everything about pop music, Dizzy," began Suzie-Q.

"Well, not everything exactly." He reappeared from behind the door. "I know a bit, I guess. Popular culture and all that!"

"Almost everything. More than we do, anyway. You're smart. You were on the road with a lot of people."

"You could have been a professor or something, so everybody says," said Nick.

Dizzy laughed and pulled a face.

"No, not a professor and certainly not in pop music. I've got a stupid pile of academic qualifications that I've never been able to do anything with, that's all. Comparative religion was my thing! I kind of fell into it from pop – you know, Flower Power and looking for the meaning of it all. Now what good are degrees in Comparative Religion in Battersea Village selling yesterday's records, apart from teaching other people about the same thing! Do you know Shakey Paul – comes in the shop sometimes? Collects old West Coast psychedelic records? He's one of the world's greatest authorities on Eskimo migration. He works the lorries usually, used to be a civil servant. Qualifications don't count for that much, you know. It's what's inside that counts." Then he added, with a glint in his eye, "That doesn't mean that you should stop training to be an engineer or that Suze should stop studying lit."

"Merlin Records, Dizzy," said Suzie-Q firmly, bringing Dizzy back. "You've got that scrap-book; we know you've got old cuttings and things. We want you to tell us everything that you know about Merlin Records, when it started, for instance, and so on. It seems to us like it's always been here, like Woolworths, but you knew all the people in the pop industry. We need to know."

Dizzy Richards went very quiet.

"What do you want all this info for? Is this to do with that Dark Side CD?"

Nick glanced at Suzie-Q.

"In a way. We promise to tell you later, really," she said. "We think there's something funny going on, but we need more information first."

64

"Who is Simon Le Mara?" asked Nick wearily.

"We know he's the boss of the company," added Suzie-Q, "but where did he come from, and who is he?"

Suzie-Q was pleading with unusual urgency. Dizzy knew them well enough: if they had made their minds up to find out something then there was no point standing in their way. He loved the opportunity to tell an occasional tale from the past too.

"This Merlin thing does seem to be bugging everybody lately," he said, as he pulled his counter stool round to the shop floor. He held his hands in front of him.

"OK. Simon Le Mara. Merlin Records. Well, perhaps I know a bit more than most people."

He pointed to a nearby browser rack.

"If you look in some of those old boxes over there, the rare section in particular, you'll find a number of albums on a record label called Upfront. Bands such as The Million Miles and Rabbit Warren used to record for them. The company was owned by a young record producer called Dan Fauster. Rumour had it that he was the real man behind a lot of big '60s bands, some say he was with the Rolling Stones until they gave him the boot. Jerry wouldn't have anything to do with him, though. Fauster was scatty. In a word, he was a nutter. He lived on his own in a round room at the top of what is now the Merlin Megastore building. He had a freaky reputation, you know, the Hermit Rich Boy thing?"

Dizzy cleared his throat.

Suzie-Q nodded. Nick listened carefully.

"Well. Dan Fauster wasn't quite that bad, but he sure did have a few odd habits that upset his staff, that's putting it mildly. I used to go with a chick that helped run his staff, chauffeur, cook, cleaner, etc etc. Jan, Jan I think her name was, before I met Meg of course. That's how I know all this. She always used to joke about the oddball gear they had to clean out of the penthouse sometimes. They found feathers everywhere once, like he'd done his own chicken plucking for dinner. You can go funny the richer you get. There was another thing; Jan used to talk about loads of deliveries of old books sometimes, from specialist book shops."

"Dirty books?" asked Nick.

"No," laughed Dizzy, "books from antiquarian dealers. Second-hand, but expensive. He was supposed to have paid a grand for one of them. He really got into this old stuff. Far worse than me and all my books. He also got permission to use a collection at the British Museum. They've got a special Reading Room there. You need a pass to get in. Nobody took too much notice – after all, he had some strange bands and we all used to reckon that he was searching for ideas for stage acts, just research. It got really peculiar, though.

"One day, right at the height of this near-success, Jan tells me that they've all been given the push and that the company was being sold to a guy called Le Mara. Simon Le Mara. It was as simple as that. Here one day

66

and gone the next. The *Melody Maker* announced that Dan Fauster had vanished off the face of the earth, gone into seclusion somewhere. There was talk of him having gone off to serve under a master, er, a guru. They were two a penny in those days, after all. It turned out that the company had been a hair's-breadth away from going under. Le Mara buying it up saved the day. My chick, Jan, had the job of getting the penthouse suite cleared up on the morning of the announcement. Dan Fauster left the place in a right state. He'd lit a fire in the middle of the lounge and the room was always hotter than hell anyhow. Loads of scorch marks on a pine polished floor, and there was another thing. Chalk and paint scrawl was everywhere, all over the walls, floors and ceilings."

"What did it say?" asked Suzie-Q.

"Nothing," said Dizzy.

"Nothing?" Nick frowned.

"I wasn't there, of course, but according to Jan it was gobbledegook, just scribble. Anyhow, the staff were each given a huge sum to disappear and keep their mouths shut. Jan Duvet could never keep her mouth shut about anything, she blabbed to me and took off with a roadie from California. I never heard from her again."

"But who was Simon Le Mara?" asked Suzie-Q.

"Want more, eh?" said Dizzy. "Simon Le Mara came out of nowhere. A mysterious stranger. Some say he came from an electronics background, was a studio producer in Los Angeles. Interestingly, he was like Dan Fauster in many ways. Similar eccentricities. I bet you've only ever seen one or two pictures of him? Short kind of guy, I believe, with this weird goatee beard and moustache. He has a big publicity hype but it's all kind of by proxy. He rarely gets involved himself, you know that. You listen to the news, read the papers. An occasional interview perhaps. Le Mara's perfectly groovy, but with a knack for business which Dan Fauster never had. The Upfront company became Merlin. Profits soared, and all of that has happened within the past five years. It's a real success story, there're Merlin shops everywhere. He even put money into science and tech."

"How do you mean?" Nick edged towards the front of his seat.

"Dunno too much about it. He wanted to invest in the music business, but through technology: tapes, processing and the like. He was a clever guy, foresaw the rise of Pop Tech and the push-the-button brigade. He even got an award for 'Services to Industry', I think. Le Mara had a lot of fingers in different pies. Anyway, that's all there is. This is my 'get things organized' morning."

Dizzy hopped off his stool.

"Oh, there is one odd thing about the company," he added. "I don't have a listing at hand but I noticed it the other day – it's the admin centres, the regional head offices of Merlin are in some very funny places. Little villages, some of them." Dizzy wrinkled his nose. "It's nothing. Forget it, you've got to put your base somewhere, I suppose."

Nick had gone very, very quiet. Dizzy suddenly noticed how strange he looked.

"You OK?" asked Dizzy

Nick nodded.

"Hope you're not heading for this new strain of flu virus that we seem to have imported from somewhere."

"Flu virus?" asked Suzie-Q. "What flu virus?"

"Let me turn the radio up," said Dizzy, as he passed behind the counter. "It was on the television last night. Perhaps there'll be an update on the morning news. The media, bless their hearts, are calling it the Pop Bug. Seems to hit kids of your age, so be careful. It's a sudden outbreak, nothing serious but it affects everyone differently, makes you feel washed out. Doctors think it's something that's going round discos and clubs perhaps. No chance of me getting it, though!"

Nick suddenly grabbed Suzie-Q's arm.

"Listen!" he shouted.

"What's the matt . . . " began Dizzy.

The radio played a few bars of a sound both kids had heard somewhere before.

"Hi there!" said the radio voice, "Merlin Records here. We're proud to announce, at last, the best band in the world. They will be playing to a specially invited audience at the new place to be: Lasers!"

There was a synthesized bass run. A hollower voice rang out.

"They are coming. Opening night is approaching. They will be with you soon, from Dark Side Discs: The Incubi."

A network of notes tripped down into the shop.

"The Incubi?" asked Nick.

Dizzy took off his spectacles, small beads of sweat began to form and glisten on his forehead. The music was upsetting him.

"That's a funny name for a band," said Suzie-Q.

"... licking and lapping, licking and lapping ..."

The voices were sweet.

So sweet, yet from another time.

Soft, but firm notes with fine edges as sharp and clear as winter crystal. High falsettos which rang and echoed like the song of choirs in lonely candle-lit chapels.

Nick wondered where it might be coming from, at first. All this celestial beauty. It bothered and comforted him, both at the same time.

Fear and pleasure together.

Were the voices coming from next door? Downstairs? Or perhaps from out in the street? Maybe it didn't matter.

His breathing had become more difficult. That was what had woken him. The blankets were pulled up close round his neck. He wasn't sure why. He still felt drained from the encounter with track seven on the Dark Side CD. If only he could remember exactly what had happened, and why it had happened. Now he felt hot and clammy and so tired. It was as if heavy weights were pressing down upon him.

The curtains were still tightly drawn. The buzz of the street lamp outside the window was barely discernible. The orange neon glow peeped through the flimsy material below the hem.

Far away, the voices of the angels continued, but now the song was changing.

Could he hear distant thunder? Was there a storm? It was coming from the room itself, seeping slowly from the very pores of the walls.

The bedstead shook, shuddering above the castors.

It was breaking through. It was coming. The primitive beat.

The psalm-like chanting grew.

Stronger. Stronger.

Deeper voices crept their way into the harmony. Low basses which growled and suddenly rose up to meet the childlike melody line.

They crashed head on.

The discord exploded into the darkness of the bedroom. The sound dived down from out of the blackness of the four corners, swooping below and over the bed.

The twist and twang of a tightly stretched piano wire snapped inside Nick's chest. He screwed his face up tight.

Ooof. Thump.

Needle pain. Sweet yet sharp.

Crush. Thump.

Rushing river. Running away with life unspent.

Crush. Thump.

A searching tongue: licking and lapping. Licking and lapping.

Crush. Thump.

Straws that suck and feed.

Ooof. Thump.

All that weight sank between his shoulders.

He caved in.

Eyelids flicked open.

Something black, black and unpleasant.

He remembered from a long-ago dream.

Now it sat above him, a small crouching creature with red eyes, and wings, curled foetus-like, within a shelter.

Glaring down.

The weight of it crushed his bones into the mattress. Thankfully he could not make out a face. There were only small red points of light held inches away from his own. His jaw fell open. Wide open. He tried to scream, he had to scream, but his mouth was too dry and the lack of spit produced a harsh rasp that stuck at the back of his throat.

The room began to turn, spiralling round that central point, twisting and turning with the darting weave of the music. The thunder of notes grew, frantically repeating their pattern like a bizarre bolero.

A thin black outline of smooth shiny lips, like a dog's, parted beneath the red eyes. A dark oval, filled with pearl, opened into an awful circle.

Licking and lapping. Licking and lapping.

Lapping and lapping and lapping and lapping and . . .

"Are you good enough?" A voice breathed the question into his right ear.

"I'm sure you are."

From the corner of his eye he saw the drape of a jacket, a dark blue suit, a uniform. Two hands pressed firmly down on the edge of the bed. Nick's head shot round to the right. There was the smile, the peaked cap, but above all else there was the thick scar which divided the face of the Guardian into two.

Nick caught his breath. It choked him.

At the line of the scar, the face began to fold and curl away, perfectly dividing itself like a carefully peeled piece of fruit, right down the middle.

Something crouched inside.

"No! Pleeease no!"

Ooof. Thump!

Nick sat upright with a cry, his hands tore away the sweaty tangle of bedclothes which had tied themselves round him.

He was soaking, his T-shirt stuck fast to his back. The struggling afternoon sunlight penetrated the point where the curtains met. His trembling hand reached out to the bedside table. There was some orange juice left in a glass. The digital radio alarm said 15.00.

He had slept through.

Nick sat on the edge of the sofa. He'd stopped shaking. Several jugs of coffee and a cold shower had helped. The note from his mother was still perched on the mantelpiece behind the vase. She'd "thought it best to let him have a lie-in. He hadn't been looking well. Perhaps he had the flu bug that was going round. Stay out of those disco places," the note had said. "Don't go into college today."

He didn't bother to dry his hair properly.

Usually he would spend hours on it, producing a work of art with hair gel and egg white. Perfecting the black spike. Now it simply sat back from his forehead. Flat and lifeless. It was an outward thermometer, looking like he felt.

What bugged him most was being unable to remember anything. That, and feeling so tired, so washed out. After Suzie-Q had found him perched against the furniture muttering numbers and things about Merlin and Lasers, she had tried hard to take him back through the series of actions. What was it that had floated out of the CD drawer? Patches of memory occasionally flashed through his mind. He remembered voices whispering hard into his ear, and rays of silver light were everywhere. There was some kind of animal too. That was particularly worrying – what was the animal?

He had abandoned his attempts to relax by playing with the Yamaha. Nothing would come out right. He couldn't play today. His fingers had tripped clumsily over the keys, his left hand running into his right. There had been bum notes everywhere, and in a fit of pique he had thrown the keyboard against the wall.

He sat and stared at the pile of leads and

socket boards that peeked out from under the black tower block which made up the music centre.

Merlin. Merlin. Merlin.

That was the key to it all. This was personal now, though. He would get to the bottom of it.

He cradled his fingers together and pushed hard down on his head, flattening his hair back against the scalp. He gritted his teeth. What to do?

Then he had an idea.

The girl at Merlin. The shop assistant with the pouting lips had spoken of casual jobs. They were taking people on. Shelf-fillers. He could apply and learn more about what was happening there and, maybe, what had happened to him. Suzie-Q was already carrying out investigations of her own. They could co-operate, work as a team.

His next thought was to get on the phone to tell Suzie-Q of his plan. Then he remembered she had lectures today and had said something about wanting to go to the library. She wouldn't be back until late.

He looked at the clock. It was 3.45.

Perhaps he would make it to Oxford Street. But no, wait. He might not make it in time.

Nick looked round for a telephone directory. He would ring Merlin and ask about the procedure for applications. Piles of old newspapers and magazines fell out from the telephone table shelf. Every kind of directory except the one he wanted.

Then he remembered the Dark Side CD. The telephone number might be on the disc itself. After all the label was a subsidiary of the Merlin Corporation.

The disc had been wrapped carefully in its Merlin Megastore paper bag. He had put it at the back of the tangle of leads in the bureau drawer. He suddenly felt nervous. As he reached into the drawer to retrieve the bag his hand began to quiver and shake, the ends of his fingers tingled.

This was ridiculous. It was only an album. What was there to be afraid of?

He grabbed the bag and took out the disc.

The CD slid easily out of its wrapping. He placed it firmly down on the bureau top, like the final hand in a card game.

The CD stared back.

Everyone was there.

But it had changed. Again it had changed. He was sure of it, but how? Realization hit him.

He felt sick.

The crowd was bigger. Much bigger.

There in the front row, wide-eyed and smiling, was a West Indian kid with an oversized knitted beret. He looked familiar, only the dark glasses were missing. Then he caught another face, behind the back row of figures. The hair spilled up and outwards like a black tangled plant.

Perhaps he was mistaken.

But the pit of his stomach told him.

He felt the blood drain from his face as he stared back at himself.

He had joined, it seemed.

77

"... mystical beasts..."

Pollyanna's was well packed out for a late afternoon. Despite the No Smoking sign, whorls of grey-blue smoke hovered above cubicles within which could be heard the usual student raucos. Jokes and laughter and chatter clashed with anxious guesses about what exam questions might come up for the end of term assessment. Fabio rushed around balancing empty plates on top of cups and saucers and complaining that if the kids wanted to stay then they had to buy more than just one cup of coffee.

He didn't mind, though. Not really.

The students provided his trade, the alternative place to the college canteen. In many ways it was a natural extension of the college. Posters decked the brown stained walls, advertising end of term dances, Film Society screenings and For Sale and Wanted items. An out-of-place National Theatre poster asked for names for a departmental evening out to go and see a resurrected foreign play. Not many had signed up.

In the corner of the café, an enormous ghetto blaster competed against the row. It was balanced on a stone-washed denim jacket, tightly held against an obscured head. It could have been anybody's head for all Suzie-Q cared. She was locked in a world of her own. She often went to the café when she wanted time to think, and she did her best thinking over coffee, usually by carrying on a conversation with herself.

If there was anyone she knew there she hadn't noticed, and fortunately nobody else had sat in her cubicle. So she was alone. Alone with her hurriedly collected pile of strange books.

The quest for information had taken her most of the afternoon. The college library had been pretty hopeless, but it had at least been able to provide her with a key book and at the back of that there had been a reading list. It was a start anyhow. Then she had gone to the public library round the corner.

She had been in the cubicle for a long time, possibly hours. The remains of several half-finished cups of coffee cluttered the table before her, beside the large fat volume recommended by the librarian.

Now was the time for serious research.

She took another sip of coffee and opened the book at the place she had marked with an old envelope and read the entry again. *MERLIN: See Huns; Incubi. Famous wizard, said to be offspring of an incubus and the daughter of one of the kings of Britain.*

"Offspring of an incubus," she traced the words with her finger as she read the entry softly to herself.

"What's an incubus? Something to do with wizards. Our Mr Le Mara seems to like keeping with a theme. Some kind of hang-up perhaps?"

She thought for a moment. She remembered the radio in Dizzy's shop. The new band – The Incubi.

"Plural, I suppose," she sniffed. "These names, though?"

She decided that it was not really that unusual for a company to keep a family of names for their products, however peculiar they might be. There might be other links, other connections.

She closed the book and sipped again at her cold coffee.

Looking around, she began to feel self-conscious about the titles before her, almost cranky. The librarian had certainly given her an odd look.

"What am I doing reading this lot here?" she said to herself.

She decided to put the books back in her carrier bag.

Suddenly, a hand passed in front of her and picked up the small red book which lay beside her saucer.

"*A Dictionary of Devils and Demons?* Oh yeah?

Into broomsticks, are we? And this other one, *The Fall of Camelot*? What are you up to, then?"

Suzie-Q spat her coffee back into the cup. The hand belonged to a long thin spider arm.

"Terry!" she cried. "You nearly frightened the living life out of me."

"Can I sit down?" he asked as he sat across from her without waiting for a reply.

"Of course you can. Here, don't tell anyone I'm reading this stuff, don't want people to get the wrong idea. I think I'm on the track of this Dark Side disc thing, the Merlin promotion. There's some real 'off the wall' connections. Whatever you do, don't tell Dizzy yet, you know he's funny about these things, takes it all so seriously."

Terry placed his arms in front of him. He played with the fingers of one hand, his right leg tapped out a nervous tattoo. He leaned forward. Suzie-Q thought he was about to kiss her but the lip twitched as he shot a searching glance out of the cubicle, to make sure that they were not being overheard.

"What's wrong?" she asked, unable to stand his fidgeting any longer.

"Keep your mouth shut about this, all right?"

"Eh? What's going . . . " His directness had caught her unawares, it wasn't like him.

"It's Josh."

Suzie-Q leaned further forward.

"Yes?"

"Something's happened to him. I don't know what exactly. He won't talk about it, but I know it's something to do with the Dark Side disc we were talking about at Dizzy's. He's as restless as hell, perhaps he's got this flu thing. I just dunno. We were going to meet this morning to go over a few numbers. He didn't want to know, said he'd lost interest, possibly in the whole idea of being in a band. He was pacing up and down in the kitchen like some animal. Talk about tense, the guy was really screwed up. Shit, he's real upset."

Suzie-Q shifted nervously on the seat.

"He's not on anything?"

"Drugs?" said Terry sharply. "No way. Not Josh. I know he's a bit wild sometimes but he's got more sense than that. No, it's that CD, I'm sure of it."

Suzie-Q shivered, despite the warmth of the café. Terry continued, not noticing how white she'd gone.

"When I left, I ran into Ezra out in the street, you know Ezra, Josh's kid brother. I couldn't get a lot of sense out of him. Well, who can get sense out of a kid brother, but it seems like there's a guy on the block who's got copies of this Dark Side CD and is daring kids to play it. The guy works at Merlin, in one of the offices. He's involved in some way with this promotion. Ezra said this guy had got some freebies from the store. Apparently it's hard to get copies now, but some staff can still give the odd one or two away to good musicians. Gotta be musicians."

Suzie-Q began to tap away nervously on the table, imitating Terry's agitation, but continuing to stare at him.

"Go on," she said.

"Well, Ezra thinks that this guy's on commission, the more kids he can get to listen to the CD, and get to take tickets for this club thing, then the more he gets in his pay packet. I couldn't follow it completely. Ezra reckons that Josh spent a long time locked in his room on Monday night."

"Oh God, he didn't . . . "

Terry stopped and reached out towards Suzie-Q's hands, which were now curled into a tight fist.

"What is it . . . ?"

"Go on, go on," she hissed.

"OK, hang on. Josh had been told that it was a test of real musicianship, dare he be tested, like, was he good enough or some such hype. It seems like he took the dare for some reason. You know what he's like. Sodding big-head and half a brain sometimes. He must have been crazy, especially after that bust-up in the Merlin store. Anyhow . . . "

Suzie-Q closed her eyes and bit her tongue. Josh had listened to the disc.

Terry peered over the cubicle for a moment and then continued in a quieter tone.

"Since that night he's changed. He's a different person and I'm worried."

Suzie-Q opened her eyes and looked directly back at Terry. She wondered if she should say anything about Nick. He and Josh had both heard the disc at the same time, and under the same circumstances.

She decided to keep quiet for the time being,

83

at least until she had spoken to Nick again. She would be meeting him tomorrow.

"It's probably this flu virus," she said weakly. "It's all round the college."

"Maybe," said Terry. "But I don't like any of it. What are all these books, what's this got to do with anything?"

She tried to collect the pile together again, but he grabbed one from her and flicked through the pages. Hundreds of drawings passed by: old woodcuts of spitting demons, witches on broomsticks with lists of spells, stone carved devils and illustrations from Gothic manuscripts and Books of Hours with strange mystical beasts.

"This stuff isn't going to help, not all this voodoo and magic crap," said Terry.

"But there are some connections ... really ... " She began to explain, but stopped herself. Terry was an old friend, but he'd never understand all this. She wasn't even certain that she did. He continued browsing through the pictures. Then he stopped and stared at a centre colour section.

"Look here," he said, opening one of the pages fully in front of her.

Terry pointed at two colour plates. One of them showed an anguished figure signing or turning a page in a book that was held out in front of him by a goat-headed demon. He read the caption.

"Take a decko at this, this is gruesome: *Goya: The pact with the Devil. National Gallery, London.*"

Below this was a drawing of a star, contained within a circle.

"The Pentacle – a magic star with five branches."

He continued to examine the drawing.

But it was the colour plate on the opposite page which suddenly held Suzie-Q's attention. The plate and in particular the inscription.

Her lower lip trembled. She pulled the book from his grasp and stared at the page. She felt dizzy.

She leapt up from her seat.

"I've gotta go," she said suddenly, snapping the book shut.

"Hey!" cried Terry. "What is it? What's up?"

Suzie-Q dropped the heavy volume on to the coffee cups. Her face blotched into a red fluster.

"Gotta go, gotta go," she mumbled.

She wiped her forehead while her other hand struggled to collect the books up again. She tucked her scarf into the front of her coat, hitched her shoulder bag and hurried out of the cubicle.

Fabio stood beside Terry. The café door had been left wide open.

"What's up with her?" Fabio asked, as he nonchalantly collected up the remaining cups. He was half used to students running off, late for lectures.

"I don't know," said Terry quietly. "She saw something in a book. What, though . . . ?"

". . . something had happened to their souls . . ."

Nick hesitated when he saw the crowd in front of the store. They reminded him of another, similar scene, all those figures jostling together like an assembled wedding party waiting for the photographer to take the family album shot.

The Oxford Street crowd had gathered in front of the main window of the Merlin Megastore. A kaleidoscope of different hair designs, shapes and colours bobbing here and there. Leather jackets and chains, jogging suits, old dinner jackets, a concentration of fashionable youth squeezed into one spot.

"They've brought the date forward!" Nick heard someone cry.

"My brother's got tickets. I couldn't get one anywhere!" cried another.

Nick forced his way through the frantic pedestrian traffic to the gathering. The enormous plate glass reflected back eager faces.

Smaller kids had managed to push their way to the front and were squeezing their noses against the pane.

Silver letters shimmered behind the glass, three-dimensional messages propped up amongst an ever-changing display of laser light:

THE INCUBI WILL BE WITH YOU SOON

And beside this, written on a board in imitatory handwriting:

BY POPULAR DEMAND

– OPENING NIGHT
BROUGHT FORWARD!

MUSICIANS FROM THE SHADOWS WILL
BE PLAYING AT

LASERS

APRIL 30th
MIDNIGHT

ADMISSION BY ADVANCE TICKET ONLY

ARE YOU GOOD ENOUGH?

WE SHALL SEE...

Nick tried hard to remember the date.
"It's Wednesday, isn't it?" he said under

his breath, "but what's the date and when is the 30th?"

Whenever it was, it wasn't far away. Why had they brought the date forward? Perhaps Merlin were being sussed. There had to be a connection between the flu bug and the Dark Side CD. The whole thing smelt of a plot, of conspiracy.

"I've come about the job as a browser rack-filler. I telephoned yesterday. I have an appointment."

Nick stood timidly before one of the raised INFORMATION counters which were scattered throughout the Merlin store. The octagonal shaped islands formed isolated booths of Merlin staff, safely segregated from the customers. The blue uniformed Guardians still roamed the floor with their portable radios and polished faces. Nick tried not to look at them for too long but he couldn't help himself. Where was the Guardian with the bad scar, he wondered. Did he really want to find him anyway?

"Straight through the store to the Folk and Classical section. Through the yellow swing doors marked Staff, and ask at the reception desk there."

His directions came from a tall blonde with a beehive hairstyle. Large panda eyes had looked straight through him. She was dressed completely in black, a long tight pencil-thin dress with only a large circular Merlin Badge to disrupt the continuity.

The store hummed as he moved through an ever-changing whorl of customer traffic. For all the company he felt very alone. What disturbed him most were the expressions on their faces. Ordinary West-End customers had been transformed into mindless sleep-walkers.

Drifting and buying.

Drifting and buying.

Something had happened to their souls. Greedy hands flicked quickly through browser boxes: albums, cassettes and CDs were being snapped up faster than they were being filled. The rack fillers were hardly managing to keep up with it all.

Suddenly, Nick was at the far end of the store, before the yellow swing doors.

This part of the shop seemed quieter than the rest. There were fewer customers here and the browser boxes were undisturbed, each record neatly in its correct spot. He looked back across the shop floor. It was a different world back there, as though all the hustle and bustle were some projection.

"Can I help you?" said a deep voice.

Nick turned on his heel. His heart skipped a beat.

A waxen face met his own, it had a wide grin and dark glasses with a peaked cap. But this Guardian was taller and thinner, with hollow cheeks sucked well into his face.

But there was the same scar.

In the same place.

"Are you OK? Can I help you at all?" persisted the Guardian.

Nick snapped back to life, his mouth ran.

"Shelf-filler. I'm a shelf-filler, I've got an interview here. But I'm not sure if this is the right place, I was told to ... Perhaps I should go back to ... "

"Relax, boy." The smile stretched even further, up towards the Guardian's ears. "This is the place. It's OK. Just a little informal chat with a couple of people, that's all. The Supervisor first. Come this way."

The Guardian turned briskly away, towards the swing doors. He pushed one yellow flap open. Nick went through, but the Guardian didn't follow. He allowed the flap of the door to swing shut behind him. The crash of silence was immediate.

Nick found himself in a small lobby, with a small counter before a box, styled like a railway ticket collector's booth. This partitioned the reception area from a long white corridor. A young, dark-skinned girl with a similar blue uniform to the store Guardians sat on a high stool within the booth.

"Interview. I've come for ... "

"Browser rack-filler?" asked the girl sharply.

Nick nodded.

The girl pushed a button on the top of the counter whilst rapping out a code into her hand radio.

"One moment. He'll be with you right away," said the girl. "We interview all the time."

Seconds later, a white-haired man stood beside the booth. Pasty-faced, with white bushy eyebrows and pink eyes, he looked as if he had been inserted into the smart dark pinstripe suit. It was impossible to guess his age. He had appeared from nowhere.

"Come this way, young man. I am the Supervisor. This won't take long."

Nick was taken along the main corridor. An empty stretch punctuated with windowed doors.

The Supervisor held a small disc against a special red security sensor. This allowed them to pass through.

"We seldom use keys," the Supervisor had quietly said as he noticed Nick's curiosity. "A Mega Corporation requires Mega Security."

The corridor was too white, a brilliant bleach of white with shiny ceramic floor tiles. It matched the Supervisor's albino hair. The bright yellow of the doors bounced back off the tiles like rays of sunlight. Nick felt as if he had entered a hospital.

Once through the second set of doors, they came across a clearer stretch of corridor.

The floor tiles in this section of the building were spotted with a design. Randomly set within the plain white floor were an assortment of geometrical shapes. Stars, and circles and triangles. Nick half closed his eyes for a moment. The shapes shifted into a larger pattern.

"This way, please," said the Supervisor. "My office is just through here."

They suddenly stood beside a side door. He placed his circular disc before the glowing red light. A single yellow door opened automatically. Nick entered the small cubicle of an office. There were two chairs and a single table with a backdrop of Merlin Megastore posters.

Once inside the room, with the door tightly shut, the Supervisor wasted no time.

There was no clock to be seen. Time had dissolved once Nick had passed through the STAFF ONLY section at the rear of the store. The walk to the room had seemed a very long walk indeed.

The Supervisor sat opposite Nick, hands chain-linked and resting on the edge of the nearly bare table. He began his spiel. "The standard selection procedure is in two halves. I will give you a brief history of the Merlin Mega Corporation, some handout sheets which will support this information, the conditions of employment, some simple ground rules, and then you will be directed to the Personnel dept. That will be the second half of our procedure. They will require you to answer a few simple questions on our application forms and you will be notified of your suitability. If you have any further questions about procedure, now is the time to ask them."

The Supervisor stopped the automatic speech. There was no indication of emotion, no smile or frown. It could have been a machine talking to Nick.

Nick shook his head.

"Splendid. Now to proceed."

There was a moment of throat clearing.

"The Merlin Corporation was successor to the former 1960s' record company Upfront. The previous president, Mr Daniel Fauster, sold the company to rock impresario Simon Le Mara in

1968. Mr Le Mara successfully handled many young popular music bands on his own labels: Templar and Midnight in particular. The '70s saw the company's successful transition into trading and promotion and in particular Mr Le Mara's very generous underwriting of research into digital technique . . . "

Nick's mouth went dry, a raw nerve had been touched.

"Are you all right?" asked the Supervisor.

Nick nodded.

"I shall go on then. Much of today's scientific advances in the field of digital processing is a direct result of Mr Le Mara's investment in the industry, for which Merlin received the Scientific Council's Award For Industry in 1980. Today, the company has a policy of consolidation. We have major stores around the country, of which the Oxford Street branch is the largest. We operate from six headquarters based down here in the south. Most of our investment is invisible. Mr Le Mara prefers it that way."

The Supervisor looked up as if expecting a question, but Nick remained silent.

"Our subsidiaries," the Supervisor continued, "include our new compact disc label Dark Side Discs, a chain of music clubs for today's youth. Lasers, the first, will be opening very shortly. there is also Mr Le Mara's own pet project, the sound of tomorrow today: DigiWave. It is intended that we shall be branching out next year into the personal computer market. We are already testing the market in a few selected outlets. Hi-fi systems and other forms of home entertainment will follow. Our aim is to be the largest producer in the world. The maps behind me show the location of our stores and main offices. Other information concerning the Merlin empire will be given to you before you leave. I shall be giving you hand-outs.

"Next. It is our policy that every young person should have the opportunity of employment. Mr Le Mara operates many schemes for today's youth but of course, there are only x amount of jobs to go round. For this reason we only employ on a short term basis, after which I am afraid you will be unable to work for us again. This policy is only applied to the under 21s, but it does give every young person the opportunity to work. We will therefore employ you on a restricted hourly basis for a maximum of three months. At the moment there are vacancies in the browser rack field. You will operate out in the store, and in the store only. Is that quite clear?"

The thick white bushes were raised.

"Yes," said Nick.

The bushes dropped again.

"Merlin is a very tight operation, mainly because of our investments elsewhere. I am of course talking about research. I'm sure you understand. We are a high industrial espionage risk. That is the reason for the kind of lengthy procedure which we are having to execute with you now. We also feel that a brief history and setting of context is useful for new employees."

Nick nodded, feeling somewhat exhausted from his five-minute verbal induction.

"When you report for work you will be assigned a personal contact and a code. Your precise hours will be given to you by the Personnel dept after you have completed a formal application and taken the Merlin special aptitude test. That is all. Do you wish to proceed to the second half of the selection procedure and do you have any questions?"

"No. It all sounds interesting," said Nick, rather unconvincingly. "Where do I go to now?"

"One moment," said the Supervisor. He leaned forward across his table and pushed a grey button. A small funnel appeared to rise up in front of him. He spoke into the mouthpiece.

"Browser-filler. Stage two coming through to you now. Confirm grade beta to take."

He paused. A green light at the front of the table glowed for a second.

"OK to go." The Supervisor grinned. "Between you and me, just a formality. Checking that you don't have two heads!"

He opened a folder which lay in front of him. He shuffled a few sheets for a moment and then handed them to Nick.

"Now listen carefully. You go out into the corridor and turn right through the first set of yellow doors. They will open for you and one of our friendly Guardians will be there to meet you and take you to the Personnel dept. Good luck. This interview is now terminated."

The door behind Nick opened.

He folded his hand-outs and held them tightly in his right fist. The sweat from his hands soaked the thin paper sheets. As he stepped out into the corridor, his breath left his body in a single rush. The tension had been unbearable. Part of him wanted out, but there was no turning back now.

"... Monk's music, yeah, that's it, Monk's music..."

The record shop in Battersea Village was closing up. It had been a quiet day and an earlier shut-up than usual wouldn't bother anybody. Meg had telephoned last night too: the wholefood business was booming: all sold out and she was on her way back home. That had made him happy. Meg might help normalize the present tilt of things.

Dizzy had spent most of the time sorting through his backlog of second-hand rock and roll records. He had basked in the joyful waves of memory which had swept over him during the half-hearted attempts at cataloguing. It had been difficult enough to get through even half a dozen LPs before eagerly rushing over to the old Garrard SP25 Mark II record deck.

He had to listen to that one again, and on the SP25. It made them feel at home. Modern gear highlighted the crackles, and the scratches and the pops. Old records needed to be played on old equipment.

The last bars of Rabbit Warren's hit from 1968, "CIA Rocker", had drifted away into hiss at the end of the record. Dizzy had stood in the middle of the shop, miming to Pete Johnson's dazzling guitar riff. His eyes had closed as he managed to bend a G sharp into a long, beautiful, imaginary blue wail of a note with his middle finger.

He had last heard that number at the Manchester University student sit-in. They had occupied the Registry department and the song was adopted as the student National Anthem for those glorious four weeks of peace and love and rock and roll.

The power of rock.

It could transcend anything

It could change the world.

He opened his eyes and repeated the words.

"Change the world . . . we nearly did that in the '60s, didn't we? Flower power. Psychedelia. Rock and roll. And then there was the purifying flame of punk. All vital forces. Change the world."

He let his words sink in.

"DigiWave . . . change the world . . . "

The shop door bell clanged. He had forgotten to bolt the door. Suzie-Q stood in the doorway. She had run there all the way from Pollyanna's. A pile of books were held tightly against her chest.

She looked hunted.

*

The battered red Venetian blinds were closed and the door was locked, but inside the shop the lights still blazed.

Suzie-Q had tried hard to hold the tears back as she had relayed the past couple of days to Dizzy. She was frightened now. Before, it was a mystery game, a jigsaw, but the connections were there. So obvious, and yet it was only by turning pages in a book and seeing those names together that some kind of ridiculous sense was being made of it all. She didn't understand it, but Dizzy would. He knew about these things.

She tried again to sip the hot coffee. It must have been the hundredth cup that day.

Dizzy looked more serious than she had ever seen him before. He had paced the shop floor for several minutes, not saying anything, but biting his bottom lip and scratching his head. Suzie-Q's newly acquired books were laid out on the counter, open at various spots that she had marked with pieces of exercise book paper.

"It's a gimmick," said Dizzy finally.

Suzie-Q sipped. Dizzy continued.

"It's got to be. Just like Alice Cooper with live snakes and Ozzie Osborne's old band Black Sabbath. Some groups even pretended to be into all this Devil worship business, but it was only a gag. Of course there's a continuity with the names and all that. It's good marketing and packaging: presenting an ongoing series and . . ."

He drifted off. He wasn't sure that he was convincing himself, let alone Suzie-Q.

Dizzy looked again at the pictures.

The painting which had particularly frightened Suzie-Q was a famous one, but she had never seen it before. It was by the nineteenth-century painter Fuseli. Dizzy knew it well, it was on the cover of a book of horror stories he'd been reading. It showed a woman lying outstretched on a bed, her arms draped backwards, over her head, lolling downwards towards the floor. Crouched above her was a small squat creature with pointed ears, glowing fearful red eyes and curled talons.

An incubus.

The painting was dark, deep shadows framing the scene, but to the left of the bed, peeking from behind a curtain, with nostrils flaring, was the head of a horse.

It had been the caption which had caused her to slam the book shut and to run from Pollyanna's. That and the familiarity of the words.

People believed that the night loosed a host of powerful creatures. Creatures which leapt on the sleeper's breast, crushing out human strength and will. In England such a creature was called a nightmare, in France cauchemar, in Germany Mahr, in Lithuania mara. Mara – crusher.

Dizzy looked hard at the colour plate.

"A mare. Mara. That's what scared you, huh?"

"Simon Le Mara," said Suzie-Q, looking up over the mug. "Simon the nightmare and Merlin. Incubus. Dark Side. Come on, Dizzy, what's going on? I've read bits of these books. There

100

was a magician called Simon Magus and I know now what an incubus is. It's a vampire, but not a blood sucker, it takes other things: vigour, life force, energy. It drains you, dammit! Flu! Flu, shit! I saw Terry at Pollyanna's. Josh has played that disc and now he's screwed, had it, perhaps he's got this so-called flu too."

Dizzy remained silent, he had never heard her speak like this before.

He crossed the shop floor and opened a drawer at the side of the counter. The first batch of the Dark Side CDs lay among empty cassette cases and bits of wire. He took two of them out of the drawer and laid them on the counter.

"You say that there seem to be two layers of music in this thing. One on top of the other? Intertwined?"

Suzie-Q nodded. "It's electronic music, but there's also a chanting, the kind of singing you can hear in churches: monk's music, yeah, that's it. Monk's music, psalms, and hymns, but it's all mixed in with the drums and other stuff."

"Monk's music?" said Dizzy. He paused and rapped his fingers on the counter.

"My CD player needs a new fuse, then I can give it a whirl. I may be able to get the two sounds separated, see what's actually on the disc, then we can listen to this chanting properly. It can be done with a bit of electronic gadgetry. Sparks will know how. Let me get this again: Nick listened to this one night, followed the instructions and blacked out?"

Suzie-Q nodded.

Dizzy picked up the telephone and dialled a series of figures. Suzie-Q put her cup down.

After a moment there was a clicking from the ear-piece.

"Hi, it's Dizzy Richards here. Is Nick there?"

There was a moment's silence.

"Oh, I see."

It was Nick's mother on the other end of the line.

"You're expecting him back soon. Yeah, but do you know where he is? Oh, I see now. Something scribbled on a pad." There was a pause. Dizzy straightened up, alarmed. "It says what?"

There was a problem, Suzie-Q could see it in his face.

"It says, Mer . . . you sure that it says Merlin? Yeah. There's a time there? An appointment. Looks like 3.45. Holy shit! Are you certain now?"

Suzie-Q's hand shot to her mouth.

"No!" she cried into the palm of her hand. "He's not gone there! Please don't tell me he's gone there."

Before Dizzy could replace the receiver, Suzie-Q had leapt across the shop floor and was grappling with the bolts on the door. She wrestled with the blinds which flicked and crackled around her hands.

There was a clunk as she yanked the door open.

Dizzy replaced the receiver.

"Suze! Wait a minute! Don't do any . . . "

But he was too late. The door was left wide and she had run out into the night.

He ran to the entrance, but the round blonde head was disappearing into the distance, bobbing down towards the junction.

"Damn," he said.

Dizzy quietly closed the door. He'd never catch up with her. There'd be no point anyway, too single-minded. He reclosed the blinds and returned to his counter stool.

He allowed his fingers to rattle nervously along the top of the counter. Then the rattling slowed as they continued along the plastic cover of the Dark Side CD. He looked up at the wall. On his little cork notice board, amongst all the postcards advertising second-hand gear, was a telephone number. Beneath the number was the name Sparks Ferguson – Audio Engineer. He'd be working late at the recording studios.

Dizzy reached for the phone and dialled. A few moments later he was on the phone to his friend.

"Sparks? Dizzy. I've got a job for you. Now. Yeah, it's ultra urgent, man, serious stuff. I want you to do some technical detective work on a compact disc. Yeah. You heard me, and it's important. I'll explain when you get here. By the way, bring over a spare slow blow fuse for my CD player. It's about time I listened to something other than Jerry!"

"... He was in ..."

The corridor was an empty white tube of glossed ceramic.

Nick heard the yellow door behind him click to a firm and tight close. To the right he could see a peaked cap through the two porthole windows of the central double doors. It was one of the Guardians, waiting to take him through to the Personnel dept.

One of the red doors at the opposite end of the corridor suddenly jerked open. The left half of the pair appeared to shudder backwards and forwards, as if the automatic closing mechanism was failing to connect.

Justifying his actions was easy. He couldn't go through with another interview, and the whole purpose of applying for a job with Merlin had been to get inside the place. Besides, he was on the cover of their CD now.

He glanced back to the right. The Guardian's

head had vanished and the coast was clear. With a single and determined movement Nick stuffed his papers inside his jacket and zipped up the front.

He sniffed a resolute sniff and made for the end of the corridor.

The doors rushed towards him as the click of the faulty mechanism echoed down the passage.

There was a sudden low grating noise like a disengaged gear. The door ahead jerked forwards awkwardly.

It was beginning to close, the fault had rectified.

He felt as though each movement took for ever as his body slid through the closing gap.

A clunk reverberated from over his shoulder. The doors shut tight with a final and firm thud.

He was in.

Nick couldn't believe what he had done, lunging into a lair of lions with eyes closed!

But there were no lions.

There wasn't anybody at all. He was greeted by a low electronic buzz, a sound which seemed to hang in the air like a frozen breeze.

Nick turned and looked back through one of the door's windows. The corridor was white and empty.

This section was quite different from the rest of the building.

His feet snuggled down into a thick pile red carpet. The doors had opened into a T-junction, an intersection of wider corridors, but instead of the stark tiling which had decked the previous passage there were warm terracotta walls here, with cream ceilings and runs of bright chrome spotlights.

One of the spotlights turned slowly towards him.

He dived to the floor. It was a camera too. His fingers gripped the carpet as he managed to pull himself to a point just below the rotating light.

Security, of course. They wouldn't leave expanses of corridor unmanned. He would have to be very careful.

The buzz which he had heard earlier accompanied the sweep of the light as it turned periodically to its new position. A second began to tilt and turn its face back down the corridor in the opposite direction.

He checked his timing against the period of the sweep, and moved swiftly to the corner position of the junction. This corridor was different again: there was a complex mixture of drawings: acute angles and circles on the same terracotta walls, similar to the designs on the tiles, but here it was like a long mural. Rows of mysterious closed doors also lined the run, with the familiar entry sensor devices blinking politely beside.

What if they should open?

He dare not think about it.

Nick stood up and flattened himself against the wall. It would be quite an easy matter to dodge down the entire corridor as long as he got his timing right.

The adjoining corridor suddenly sparked into

life with a busy murmur of background noise, the kind of muffled sounds that indicate the break-up of meetings within secret rooms.

Nick looked up at the lights. He would have to move now.

Taking a deep breath, he zigzagged a precarious route along the length of the corridor, past the room with the voices.

He turned the corner and ran into a face.

He gasped.

The girl with the pouting painted lips, the rack-filler from the shop floor, stood there. She had floated into his view from the right, clipboard in hand as before but with an empty look. She was somewhere else.

"You've joined," she said dreamily. "You were good enough then?"

"Listen," he quickly looked behind as the noise of the voices grew, "you've got to help me."

"All together now." She grinned stupidly. "So glad to have you on board."

She was no use. He looked over her shoulder, down towards yet another corridor.

The place was like a warren, but this time a pair of large sheet metal doors broke the monotony. It was a lift.

The girl grinned once more. She didn't know where she was. Clipped to a top pocket was a small circular disc with a red cover. It was a sensor. A key to get around the building. One of his hands pushed the girl back against the wall as the other quickly and neatly unclipped the disc.

"Hey, you can't . . . " she began.

"Sorry, needs must," said Nick. Firmly but carefully, as Dizzy had shown him, he pinched a nerve to the right of her neck.

She slumped to the floor.

Dizzy's bit of martial arts stuff had finally come in useful.

There was not a moment to lose. The shifting sounds behind the door were getting louder. It would soon be opening.

He ran towards the lift and slammed the disc on to the wall. Above him, a series of flickering numbered lights rapidly counted down from 3 to G. The numbers went as far as 9. Instead of a 10, a small metal sign with deep red lettering had been riveted on to the panel: RESTRICTED.

The door further down the corridor opened. A hand from the blue sleeve of a Guardian uniform held on to the handle. The face which appeared telescoped crazily towards him. Deep dark shades beneath a peaked cap.

"... it was opening ..."

It was the Guardian from the CD section of the store.

The face held his own for a moment. It recognized him. The moment seemed for ever. The lift was a long time coming.

Nick beat his fist against the lift doors. "Please don't let there be anybody in there! Quickly!"

"Oi! You there!" yelled the Guardian, as he began to advance down the corridor.

The lift doors opened with a polite sweep just as the light above glowed G.

Nick leapt into the cabin and pushed his thumb on to the button marked CLOSE. There was only one direction that he could take. He squeezed the button hard against the panel until he thought that every drop of blood might seep from his flesh.

The doors rolled shut.

Without thinking he hit the top button. Get as

far away as possible, choose the farthest point.

The robotic twang of a voice suddenly cut in above him.

"Restricted Entry. Special code. Enter or abort."

Two lights blinked at him on a bright liquid LED side screen. He pushed the button next to "abort", and then pressed the number below the top button.

Number 9 glowed.

There was a thud on the door.

A muffled voice came from the other side, but it was too late.

There was a momentary shudder from way above. The ceiling pulley gears whirred into action.

The lift began to move.

Nick's knuckles practically pushed through the skin of his left fist. His other hand spread across the buttons on the control panel like an enormous fat spider. His thumb pushed hard against "Door Close" as his middle finger kept rat-a-tat-tatting away at the number 9 button.

There was a trick to it.

Some of the third-year engineering students at the college used it to bypass floors if they wanted to get to the student canteen quickly. He'd been taught the technique by Jacko, a pulleys engineer whizz kid who was doing the same electronics option as he was.

Most of the time it worked, at least in the college lifts. He prayed that it wouldn't let him down this time.

He checked the cabin's progress through the floors.

It was a fast lift, but to Nick the journey upwards was taking a lifetime. He held his breath each time the light left a floor number, his finger increasing the rhythm.

3 . . .

4 . . .

5 . . .

The lift mustn't stop.

It was working.

He'd buy Jacko a drink if he ever got out.

6 . . .

"Keep going, come on, come on!"

7 . . .

There was a sudden jolt.

The cabin heaved to one side. Nick was thrown to the floor. Above him, a metallic crash echoed up and up, bouncing its way towards the ceiling of the lift shaft. There was a crunching of gears, a tightening of cables.

The cabin had ground to a halt.

Nick scrambled to his feet and resumed his frantic beat on the control panel buttons. Nothing happened, the lift had jammed.

"Damn! The panel's been over-ridden!" he yelled.

There might be another way.

His tongue clicked nervously.

Nick felt in his pocket for his key chain, a penknife, some tool, anything to prise open the panel door.

Above him he heard the sound of a creaking door, then a dull clunk. Somebody was trying to come down the shaft.

The panel had a thin metal strip for a border.

His fingers pulled at the edging, trying to prise the lower lip off. It could be possible to fashion a temporary screwdriver and get inside to the box of tricks itself. The guts of the thing might be the same that Jacko had messed around with.

His fingertips bled as he scraped and pulled at the strip.

"Keep calm," he said to himself. "Pretend you're on a practical exam."

Then he noticed the small red sensor beside the emergency stop button. It could only be another admission switch; they seemed to be standard for the building.

He fumbled inside his jacket pocket for the sensor.

After a moment of wrestling with a handker-chief, his fingers found the disc.

The cabin shook again. Something heavy had landed on the lift roof. There was the clean clear snap of a thrown catch.

Nick's hand quickly withdrew from his pocket, he slapped the disc against the red light and pushed the button at the back. The panel gently clicked open and swung out-wards to reveal a familiar board of switchgear components.

He raised his head to heaven.

"Matthews & Johnson standard. Thank you, thank you!"

The trap door in the ceiling of the cabin shifted suddenly to one side.

Nick looked up.

Outlined against the beam of a floodlit shaft,

hovering there silently like a huge praying mantis, was the angular outline of the Guardian. He was waiting.

The teeth cracked apart across the jaw into a dreadful grin.

Nick slammed his right fist back, hard against the wall – a mixture of desperation and frustration.

The echo returned outside, in the lift shaft.

"I've been looking for you, sonny." The voice was tough.

Nick threw himself against the opposite wall of the cabin as hard as his strength would allow. His shoulder crunched into the thin aluminium casing, which buckled under the force. Above him the twang of cable spat its angry reaction down into the ringing shaft.

The cabin jolted.

The dark shape was thrown off balance.

"Heyyy, whoooa!!"

A flood of light shot through the trap door as the Guardian fell to one side. There was now a clear view up to the cable gear and the emergency halogen floods. A claw of fingers gripped the edge of the opening.

The Guardian was still there, hanging on.

Nick's action had bought him a few moments of time.

As the Guardian tried to regain his hold, Nick's hands dived inside the control panel.

He searched for the toggle connectors. *If* they were in there and *if* he could locate them.

His middle finger discovered a slide control.

A hand gripped his jacket shoulder.

He pulled back and slammed against the cabin wall again. The Guardian was halfway through the hatch by now, attempting to manoeuvre himself into a position where he could drop down into the cabin. Nick watched his own tiny distorted image in the eyeshades.

Suddenly, he made a Tai fist. With everything he could muster he thrust the clench of muscle and bone into the Guardian's face.

With a cry the Guardian pulled back, his left hand shooting up in front of his glasses. The shades shattered into cracked blackness.

Nick followed this through with a dive across to the opposite wall. With his hands hooked in front of him, he rolled his body around the cabin walls. He spun and spun. The lift shook as his weight rocked the cabin from side to side. The thudding echo telegraphed along the cables, up towards the dark ceiling.

Nick rushed to the control panel. He now knew where the over-ride was. He clicked the slide over.

The lift started to move upwards.

He looked back to the hatch. The Guardian's face reappeared. He looked larger than before. The whole body was stretched across the opening.

Nick turned to the panel. There was a circular control marked INCREASE-DECREASE. He turned it to maximum and flicked the over-ride for the top floor.

There were sparks for a moment, and a small lap of flame flickered out from the switchgear.

The cabin shook.

The Guardian rolled over on to his side. He crooked one arm under the lip of the roof opening.

The pneumatic action was immediate. With sudden acceleration, the cabin shot upwards towards the top of the shaft.

Nick's mouth gaped open.

Beyond the crooked shape of the Guardian, he saw the hard angled girders of the pulley gear. They were heading straight towards them. The brakes had been bypassed.

There was nothing he could do. He held on tight to the hand-rail.

There was a crash of metal. Sparks showered down, followed by a dreadful soft thud.

Nick was thrown to the floor.

The lift was still.

Nick looked up.

His eyes grew as every repulsive detail revealed itself, slowly and carefully like the opening bud of a flower.

The remains of the Guardian's glasses fell from his face as he let out a gargled cry. Two glowing points of fire looked out from within empty holes.

The eyes stared down at Nick.

They were somehow familiar.

Nick crouched in the corner of the lift, helplessly staring back. The corners of the cabin converged, shifting into a crazy pattern. His hand reached out to the lift wall.

The lift had crashed into the buffers. It hung from the pulley gear, locked within the tight confusion of cables.

For a moment there was only silence, but there followed a crackle and a crunching like the slow breaking of eggshells.

Nick noticed for the first time that the Guardian appeared to be suspended, floating mysteriously above the hatch. Then the tunic buttons of the uniform snapped open. The light blue denim shirt beneath revealed a growing black stain which stretched outwards across the chest like an ugly ink blot.

The end of the girder burst through the chest, the limp and useless jawbone cracked as a black trickle collected at the corner of the mouth.

The scar line which ran from the nose to the hairline became an angry orange. A fissure, like the thinly drawn zigzag of a crayon, had cut a path down the centre of the mark.

It was opening.

The head was pulling apart like an opening zip.

Nick was spellbound. Something was struggling to get out from the Guardian's body.

The red pinpoints shifted from the dark sockets. The face flexed. Curled talons appeared through the widening crack at the top of the head. It was like the crinkle of burned paper as the flesh peeled back. As though it were a carefully removed rubber mask, the skin fell away.

The body shook with a violent spasm. A wet bundle of thick black fur peeked up through the Guardian's head, black folds of skin fluttered.

Another wail gushed from the mouth, like

the scream of an animal in pain. The black shape within fizzled into blackness. The sticky liquid dripped out of the body, across the face, collecting at the chin before continuing downwards to the floor of the cabin, making a hideous skein like tangled plastic thread.

The Guardian's body collapsed into a flat, punctured balloon and flopped down on to the floor of the lift at Nick's feet.

He could now see clearly through the hatch. The shaft lamps still burned brightly. There was silence.

The broken steel girder protruded down into the lift from the crumpled pulley hoist. No blood stained the floor. There was just a pool of liquid night.

"It must have gone straight through the heart," whispered Nick to himself, "straight through the heart . . ."

"... that's rock and roll for you ... it can change the world ..."

Dizzy Richards clicked the radio tuner off and looked over at the old Memorex tape calendar which hung from the cork notice board. He had been thinking hard. Trying to make a pattern, he didn't like how the picture was shaping up.

The Merlin advertisement had been on twice that evening, accompanied by the sound of DigiWave. They were pushing it now. He had tried to listen to the music more closely this time. The kids were right, there was something there, a chant, a madrigal maybe or even a mantra. What bothered him more than anything was that the rhythm, the regularity of the beat was somehow primitive. It had an infection that belonged to states of trance, to reverie, to mysticism. To magic.

Of one thing he felt certain. Whatever it was, it was bad.

The date for the opening of Lasers had been

brought forward. "The thirtieth of April", the voice on the radio had just said.

"But of course it had to be," said Dizzy to himself, "that or one of the other nights set aside in the Witches' calendar. But the thirtieth! *The* night. Walpurgis Night. The traditional time of the Black Sabbath."

He thumped the counter and laughed. There was hysteria in his voice.

"Is this really happening?"

He thought over recent events again. CDs – they looked like mirrors. Suzie-Q had compared it to a powder compact and then one had shattered in his hand just like glass. Mirrors had power. They could capture your soul, according to certain religions and folklore. He remembered reading that when the plague crawled across Europe in the Middle Ages, mirrors were turned to the wall if someone in the household died. Broken mirrors meant seven years' bad luck. Mirror magic even had a name: catoptramantics. If magic was involved somewhere then the silver reflection of the compact disc was a perfect vehicle.

"Mirror magic . . . I wonder . . ." he said quietly.

"Talking to yourself, Diz?" said a voice. "We all know you're bleedin' barmy."

Sparks Ferguson stood at the back of the shop. Dizzy looked up, startled at first, but then he smiled at the familiar unkempt appearance of his friend.

Sparks and Dizzy went back a long way. They had played together.

"Back door was unlocked as usual, saves me going the long way round with these bloody one-way systems. Got me van, see. You'll get done one day, all this gear."

Sparks's toothless grin was some reassurance of sanity.

"Here y'are, one slow blow fuse. Gotta shift, though, if yer want this CD thing back tonight. Where is it, then?"

Dizzy took the fuse from Sparks and opened the drawer in the counter. The Dark Side CD sat there. He had removed the sleeve. He couldn't bear to look at it. He thought he might be starting to imagine things.

He handed it to Sparks, who stuffed it nonchalantly into his overalls pocket.

"I'll do me best, Diz, should get yer good results, though. Got this new graphic equalizing phaser gear at the studio. It can split off a baby's fart if it's there in the music."

"Listen to me, Sparks." Dizzy looked severe. "There's two pieces of music in here, one transposed on top of the other, I think, but I've not given it a proper listen myself yet."

He held up the fuse.

"I've needed this. There's something on that disc called DigiWave."

"Digi what?"

"On the CD . . . It doesn't matter. What does matter is that I want you to separate the vocal section. It's a choral piece, if I'm not mistaken. Then drop a cassette of it back here. OK? I'll be here all night. Meg ain't home yet. Get the tape back ASAP. It's urgent!"

Sparks stared at Dizzy. The man was usually calmness personified. Now he was agitated, fidgety and so uptight.

"OK, Diz," said Sparks quietly, "no sweat. I'm your man, but I can't guarantee tonight, maybe tomorrow morning."

Dizzy patted Sparks on the shoulder as they made their way back through the shop.

"Sparks?" Dizzy called after him.

"Yes, mate?"

"The '60s were good times, weren't they?"

"Sure were. Why?" Sparks stopped for a moment as he opened the door.

Dizzy looked strangely sad.

"Thought we could change the world, didn't we?" he said.

"But that's rock and roll for you," laughed Sparks. "It can change the world. These politicians have got it all wrong, you know, forget the old chat, use a bit of the muse. Tomorrow belongs to the young. It always has done. Jus' 'cos our scene couldn't manage it doesn't mean that something else won't do it one day. Something will come along. Mark my words. See yer later, Diz, deep natter some other time, if yer in the mood!"

Sparks vanished through the door with a casual wave.

"Something will come along . . ." repeated Dizzy. "Perhaps it has already."

"... he had stepped back in time ..."

Nick had expected alarm bells, but there was no noise of any kind after the crash. There was no sign of anybody at all. It was peculiar.

He had been quick to clamber out of the lift. The black pool which had been the remains of the creature had simply fizzled out of existence, like foaming bleach on a stain.

Once hooked up on to the roof, it was a simple matter to climb over to the emergency ladder which ran the length of the lift shaft. Directly opposite, where he now struggled to gain a foothold, large white letters were painted on the brickwork: PENTHOUSE. RESTRICTED ACCESS AREA.

He looked below him.

The shaft stretched down like a narrowing funnel. The lift had smashed past the ninth floor trip mechanism, crashing through to the top floor. Above him, beside the ladder, was a pair of lift doors, tightly shut behind rows of crossed iron railings. There was a double seal.

He clambered up past the lift doors, practically to the very top of the shaft itself. Restricted or not, every shaft had to have maintenance access to the pulley drive. He was counting on it. He searched for the familiar grid opening beside the huge wheels, and, after a moment, he found it – the trap hatch for the workmen.

It was already unlocked.

He swung himself over from the ladder and squeezed through into a dark passage. He presumed this to be the central air-conditioning duct, and the draught confirmed it. The layout seemed standard office-block installation, as studied at college. Even millionaire recluses needed basic millionaire facilities.

The passage was narrow, but at the end was a thin wedge of light. This would be the top floor. He was there. The headquarters of Simon Le Mara.

He edged his way along towards the end.

Once out into the corridor, Nick had expected to be greeted by bright lights and at least an army of people asking what he was doing there. But there was no sign of anybody at all. Occasional wall lights and paint-splattered bulbs hung from frayed flex fittings.

Paint-blistered walls were draped in stretches of cobwebs. It was as if the top floor of the building had been vacated in a hurry. There were odd scraps of carpet tile and posters which advertised old albums and concerts at the Roundhouse and Middle Earth. All dated from the 1960s.

A dusty newspaper blew in front of him across the unswept floor. He caught it with his foot. *Daily Mirror 1968*. The headlines said something about LSD and a police raid.

He realized what it all was. He had stepped back in time. This floor hadn't been touched since the 1960s.

Suddenly he noticed a door up ahead, a cracked plastic sign swung down from a single screw. Cautiously he made his approach.

The sign was covered in grime. He tried to wipe away some of the dirt with his sleeve. The words slowly appeared:

DAN FAUSTER: PRIVATE.

Nick recalled Dizzy's story. Fauster was the previous owner of the Merlin Empire. He listened at the door for a moment and then felt for the handle. There were none of the security sensors here. This floor was another world.

The door creaked open. He peered in.

It took him a moment to adjust to the dark. But he was confident that the room was empty. It hadn't been used for a long time. The lights of London flashed occasionally through portico windows which surrounded the walls. The place was large, bare and perfectly round, with a huge dome above.

Nick stepped in, pulling the door quietly behind him.

He looked up. The partial crescent of the

evening moon began to move into view through a central aperture, bringing a cast of moonglow into the centre.

Now he could see better.

Old splashes of white paint spoilt what might have been a good quality pine floor. In the middle were scorch marks, as if a fire might have been lit there once. Nick frowned at the markings. Chalk and paint, probably put there a long time ago, but the tell-tale signs were still intact. More triangles and circles like those on the tiles and on the walls downstairs.

He crossed to the scorch marks, observing for the first time a broken white line: it surrounded him like a large circle.

He suddenly spun round on his heels.

There were voices. They came from the corridor outside.

He turned towards the door. Was somebody going to come in?

The lever handle moved as a small crack of light appeared.

Nick rushed over and flattened himself against the wall. He moved round to the side of the door. His heart thumped hard. A low wheeze of words came from what sounded like an older man.

"This is the room for the equipment. Mr Le Mara has already installed the necessary aerial above the dome. Nobody is to enter this room once the link-up is established. Those taken by the disc shall have been herded together. Tomorrow night will confirm the course. Tomorrow night is the time."

"Good," said a younger voice. "Are you good enough to join?"

The older voice laughed.

The pair broke into further guffaws as the door was closed once more and echoing footsteps took them down the corridor.

Nick felt unwell. What did they mean? "Herded together"? He had a terrible feeling that he had joined this club already. What was going to happen to him, to others?

He pressed his ear hard against the door, to make sure that the footsteps really had vanished.

He had to get back to the lift shaft and out into the air duct. It was the only sure way of escaping from the building.

He reached out to the handle but before his fingers could touch the lever the door suddenly swung open.

A uniformed figure, with black shades and a peaked cap, stood in the doorway. There were two other figures behind him, Nick was unable to see their faces.

"I thought so. He's here. Nothing messy. Mr Le Mara said so."

Nick felt his legs weaken.

". . . too old, too old, too old . . ."

"Oh Suzie-Q, oh Suzie-Q,
  Oh Suzie-Q, I love you, my Suzie-Q,
  I love the way you walk,
  I love the way you talk,
  My Suzie-Q!"

Dizzy sat upright on his mattress, which was leaning in an L shape against the wall behind the counter. It was unusual for him to stay down in the shop so late but there were things to do, and a delivery to wait for.

Jerry Lennox played on in the background as usual. It was "Suzie-Q", Jerry's personal favourite hit.

The old SP25 Mark II record deck just about managed to turn the record round. Jerry's voice wowed and fluttered as the stylus moved towards the end of the disc, but then the newly readjusted auto-changer would engage a little too early and start the record over again.

Another copy of the Dark Side CD lay on the floor in front of Dizzy, next to his bag of screwdrivers, pliers and screws. Sparks's slow blow fuse had been inserted into the CD player, but he didn't want to play the Dark Side CD. Not yet.

He wondered about his reluctance. Perhaps he might even be afraid.

Dizzy was worried for life and limb now. Nick's mother had telephoned the shop twice, asking after Nick; he should have been home hours ago. They'd tried the Merlin store too, but there was always an unobtainable or engaged tone. The store would be closed anyway.

He clambered to his feet. The moment could not be put off any longer. It was time to listen to the disc.

He checked that the ill-fitting blinds were as tightly shut as he could manage before crossing over to the hi-fi gear. The lights were turned down low. He decided to listen through the headphones, it would save him having to mess around with leads and adapters at the back of his old, but faithful, Teleton amplifier. Sparks had had to rig up a special junction box for him to be able to use the CD player. Sparks had shaken his head from side to side and said something about the "attenuation" being wrong and "why didn't he get himself a decent modern amp anyway".

When the black box worked it worked well, though. Sparks was good. Dizzy hadn't understood what all the fuss was about.

He plugged his headphones into the front of the compact disc player and held the silver disc before the CD tray. The sparkle had gone from the surface; perhaps it was a trick of the light, but it looked in parts as black as vinyl.

It was now or never.

Dizzy put the CD on to the tray and pushed the red button on the player. Obediently the tray withdrew, taking the disc into its body, like a tongue taking food.

"Suzie-Q" thundered on.

He watched with attentive fascination as the bright amber LED numbers flickered across the little read-out screen. A gentle tinkle came from the player; he could just about hear it, but within the headphone pads there remained an inky black silence.

A red light glowed for a moment on the player's panel, beneath the word **ERROR**.

Dizzy pushed the "play" button again.

The tinkling of the disc was repeated, but it was faster this time.

ERROR blinked back at him again.

Dizzy unhooked his headphones, and rested them on his neck.

"Bloody technical stuff," he muttered as he reached for his batch of user manuals, stuffed on a shelf beside the amplifier.

The instructions for the player were very clear and easy to understand. It took him only a few moments to find the relevant section. He read down the list under the heading "Trouble-shooting".

"**ERROR**: The disc is unable to be read. It

may be damaged, or need cleaning. Withdraw from the tray and retry."

Dizzy pressed the "eject" button again and waited for the tray to redeliver.

The disc reappeared. He held it up to the light.

The CD looked OK but it felt strange, soapy, kind of damp. He reached out for a record cloth and wiped the surface with a couple of sweeps.

He replaced it in the tray and settled his earphones back on his head. He pressed the button again.

The tinkling sounded louder than ever this time.

ERROR blinked back at him.

He pressed "RETRY".

ERROR. He fixed the LED read-out with a firm stare.

"RETRY".

ERROR.

This time he held his finger on the button.

ERROR flashed angrily back at him.

He lost his temper.

"Come on, you son of a . . . "

From somewhere within his headphones Dizzy heard a voice. An angry spit of words at first.

"Enough taken . . . this time. Don't you understand, OLD MAN?"

Dizzy held the button down hard.

"Won't you learn, fool? We want young souls. This is not for the likes of you!"

He heard nothing further for a moment. He thought that it had switched itself off. But then, from out of the silence, it came. Unannounced and unexpected: a solid plug of digitized signal which crashed into his head, filling both ears.

He cried out in pain.

The ripple of artificial notes drilled through his eardrums, out into the cavern of his mouth.

Dizzy staggered back, hands lashing out to steady himself. He was becoming a living loudspeaker.

A growling hollow voice raced around the inside of his head.

"Too old, too old, too old!" it sang. "Enough taken! We want youth, youth, youth!"

He grabbed the headphones and tore them off his head. They fell to the floor. The musical bedlam screamed from the ear-pieces and out into the shop.

Dizzy grabbed the counter as he reeled backwards. His ears rang.

The headphones wriggled before the shop counter like a pair of wrestling eels. The ear-pieces twitched with the beat, there was a cackling voice. Suddenly they began to change shape. Dizzy watched in horror as they fizzled and melted into something round and wet and deep red which pumped with the tempo of his own pulse. He heard a voice from behind him.

"Take heart, old feller!"

"God almighty!" cried Dizzy as his arms swept out. His back hit the counter.

His shaking hands reached down, blindly searching for the amplifier's volume control. He turned the large silver control. The SP25 was still playing: Jerry Lennox sang more softly.

"Shit. It's not fixed up properly. The box!"

His fingers grappled behind the amp, searching for Sparks's black box. He felt something solid with leads coming out from the back. Not knowing precisely what he should do, he did everything. He flicked a switch and turned a dial marked CD-Record Deck.

There was a squeal, a mixture of electronic howl and animal pain. The angry squawk shot out into the shop.

The CD player beat against the shelf with a life force of its own. Then the disc tray shot open, smoke billowing from the ventilation holes at the sides. The silver disc had become a pitch black tar, dripping from the CD tray like dark, melting chocolate.

A grin of realization spread across Dizzy's face. He couldn't help it. So simple. It was almost a sign from the gods.

He danced from one foot to the other.

He had accidentally connected the CD player signal directly into the record deck. The Dark Side CD was coming straight down the signal lead and smack into Jerry Lennox, and it didn't like it. It didn't like it at all.

The SP25 Mark II turntable continued to revolve.

Only the word **ERROR** remained on the CD player for a few moments, before the whole mess clotted into a thick mass.

The disc was dead.

But "Suzie-Q" played on.

"... the crumpled face of an old alchemist ..."

Suzie-Q stood on the corner of Charing Cross Road, across and down from the flickering neon lights of the Merlin Megastore.

The busy London traffic continued to roll, despite the closing shops. People hurried home. Behind the store windowpanes of Merlin she watched as the "night light" settings switched over from the bright spot floods that usually picked out the record racks and other displays.

In the main window the date 30th April loomed large. Chalked up on the glass itself, in addition, were the words: COMING SOON TO LASERS.

She had arrived too late, all the remaining customers were leaving. The Guardians had been hopeless, not even bothering to listen to more than half a sentence. They wouldn't let anybody in.

"Company rules, once the late bell has gone. Come back tomorrow, love."

She chewed at the end of the roll of leaflets. They had been thrust into her hand outside the store front by a young Asian guy. She still held them fast in her fist.

She gazed upwards, scanning the vast building up towards the evening sky. It had to be the largest store in Oxford Street, it was certainly the tallest.

Beyond the skyline of the rooftops of neighbouring shops, a huge modern extension had been built, slightly to the rear of the frontage. Further floors advanced upwards. Dizzy had said that Dan Fauster had managed to finance it from the USA, a Yank company had got the contract and there had been a lot of rumpus over planning permission. But many hands had been greased, so Dizzy had told her.

"You're in there, Nick. I know it," Suzie-Q spoke into the roll of leaflets.

She sighed. She felt so helpless – lost and useless.

She sniffed back a tear.

"Get yerself a nice drop of coffee and a MacDougal's Burger. Things will seem better then, mark my words, love."

She turned round to see a cheerful newspaper vendor, a half-lit cigarette hanging out of the side of his mouth as he dished out evening newspapers to Underground passengers.

She looked at her watch; it was past teatime.

Perhaps it wasn't a bad idea. Time to think again. What else could she do? After all, she always did her best thinking over coffee.

The hamburger still sat in the centre of her plate, the cheese no longer soft and runny. Suzie-Q simply didn't feel hungry, but she was grateful for the coffee.

There were few people in the place, unusual for a normally busy West End burger bar. She unrolled the hand-outs, wondering why she hadn't chucked them into the nearest rubbish bin. There was the usual cut price language school offer, and an invitation to a late disco and a sale at Selfridges, but she dropped the final folded sheet as if it were burning paper.

A familiar wizened wrinkled head with the crooked eye smiled out at her. Merlin!

Seeing the face so unexpectedly had chilled her bones. She gulped back a mouthful of coffee. It was only a hand-out.

She read on. It was the first Merlin hand-out she had seen.

It appeared innocent enough. Folded into a leaflet was a two-page listing of special sale stock set in two columns. The rest of the leaflet contained the usual advertising stuff for the store. Mega this, Mega that, special video offers, T-shirts and so on.

It was the back page that held her interest.

Below yet another Merlin logo was a map of Great Britain. A series of blue dots marked the locations of the major Merlin megastores. Red markings showed the sites of the head offices. Underneath all this, set within their own box, were the addresses and telephone numbers of each store, and near the bottom were the addresses of the head offices.

Suzie-Q stared at them for a long time. She had never seen the names listed before. It was the locations which puzzled her. She remembered that Dizzy had mentioned it too: London, (well, that was an obvious place for a head office), Cambridge, (OK), Aylesbury, (that was an odd choice), Petersfield, (she had to think about that, she wasn't certain where it was), Hastings, (were there any big concerns in Hastings?) and the final place she had never even heard of except that it was in a stretch of water east of Chelmsford – Agrippa Island in the River Blackwater.

Suzie-Q found herself starting to giggle quietly.

"The River Blackwater? A mega corporation with a head office on an island? Come on, now."

She took a swig of coffee and held the map up in front of her. Her vision blurred. She was thinking so hard, the blue and red spots danced across the page.

"There's a reason, there's got to be: an odd-ball, off-the-wall reason for it. Do they have something in common? I mean, if you had a huge mega corporation concern like Merlin, would you put a head office in Hastings and Aylesbury and in the middle of a river, for God's sake?"

She thought hard. History? Was it to do with history? And there was the magic thing, too.

She stared out in front of her. Her voice had been rising and others in the bar were jerking their heads in the direction of her table.

"There's a round church in Cambridge," she said to herself, "we saw it on a school visit to the colleges." She half closed her eyes, remembering. "I think there's one in Hastings too. There's loads in London, and . . . "

"Round! Round, round!" she cried out excitedly. One of the waitresses glanced up from sweeping the floor.

Her fingers froze around the edges of the paper.

"Dan Fauster. Dizzy said that Dan Fauster had a round room at the top of the building. He lived there. Circles. It's probably still there, right up there at the top of the Merlin Megastore! Hastings . . . there's one there too, an old Templars cave on the cliff near the old smugglers' hideout!"

The red spots on the map seemed to burn, to glow like animal eyes in the night.

If only she had her books with her. Only a bit more information and . . .

Her gaze busily shifted round the room and stopped suddenly.

She felt weak.

One of the National Theatre posters was stuck in the front window of the café section. It had been all over London, down in the Underground, on the backs of buses, one of the lecturers at the college had even organized a college trip and she'd put her name down to go! She'd even read up on the play herself. This new production was opening at the Olivier Theatre.

137

A modern version of the Goethe play: *Faust,* about a man who sold his soul.

The crumpled face of an old alchemist looked out from the centre of a magical ring. He reminded her of Merlin.

She knocked her plate off the edge of the table. As if in a trance she walked across to the poster and ripped it off the glass.

"Dan Fauster. The man who vanished . . . "

It was all she could say.

138

"... smack in the centre ..."

Suzie-Q thought she was floating. It felt very pleasant to begin with. There was a warm comforting cushion of air beneath her which rolled and turned her body. First this way, and then that, the horizon of the earth tilting with the direction of the "magic carpet" current.

But the breeze blew harder, becoming more like a wind.

Her heartbeat was louder now. It had grown with a great strength, starting within her chest, but now moving upwards to a place inside her head.

A low and syrupy sweet voice whispered in her ear.

"Come, come and join us, come, come and join us ... "

It trailed off with a snigger.

The steady thud of her heart thumped on; she rose and fell with the beat.

139

The voice returned, but this time it was not alone; there were layers of words hissing at her, one behind the other. A gauze of sounds that shimmered.

"Come, come come."

" . . . And join us . . . yes, yes, yes, yes, YES!"

"You could be . . . "

"One of us . . . us, us, us, us, us, us, us . . . "

There they were, below her.

The Dark Side crowd looked up, clustered together in a tight group, yet in the centre of a vast empty space. Beckoning looks and curled fingers pleaded with her to come down from out of the sky and be with them, safely in their midst.

She saw Nick. He was standing at the back of the group. He was laughing and pointing, but at what?

The cry of the wind subsided and she began to drop. She felt that she was beginning a downward sweep. Like a bird, she stretched out her arms in a vain attempt at imitating wings, but she was spiralling downwards fast.

Suzie-Q closed her eyes, she was going to crash into the crowd. As the current suddenly caught and lifted her back upwards, she opened her eyes again and noticed what Nick was pointing at.

The group was packed into the centre of a white ring. The circle appeared to be dissected into equal parts. She recalled the cover of the Dark Side CD. "White markings, like an airport runway?"

But . . . it wasn't a runway.

The poster for the *Faust* play spun before her. The Ancient Star of the Pentacle.

They were all standing in the middle of it.

The circle spun upwards, seemingly through the crowd. A spinning silver disc sucked her in. Faster and faster. Faster and faster. A liquid silver pool, moon milk, molten magic.

A ragged claw of a hand suddenly shot out of the pool and grabbed her by the throat.

"ARE YOU GOOD ENOUGH?" demanded a voice.

Suzie-Q's face turned into her pillow. It muffled her voice for a moment as she called out, startled and afraid.

The table lamp still glowed and the clock said 3.00 am. She pulled herself up against the pillows, her nightshirt was wringing wet, the sheets wrapped around her legs. Outside the night breeze mocked her memory of the dream.

She recovered quickly. There was no time to be afraid, there was too much to think about. Her mind buzzed with activity – with strange thoughts and notions. There was now so much evidence, almost too much information. Suzie-Q was riding on a high, answers were coming to her in dreams. It was as though she had suddenly found a guide. She reached over to the bedside table for the Merlin hand-out. Her finger traced the locations of the head offices. There was something about the red spots of colour, but she couldn't be sure what.

Something about where they were on the map. It was a puzzle and the solution was contained in the dream.

It nagged at her.

She had an idea. Among the clutter on her shelves there were still some reference books, kids' encyclopaedias and dictionaries and some of Dizzy's books. She wanted Dizzy's old AA map book.

Her eyes read the titles, squeezed between boxes of board games and a stack of record albums. There was a bonus. Beside the *AA Book of the Road* was the Dennis Wheatley *Book of Magic and Mystery*. She had forgotten she had this.

Suzie-Q pulled the scruffy black book from out of its case.

"Pentacle . . . Faust . . . "

Her fingers ran through the index.

"No Faust. Try Pentacle."

There was an entry; she read the words slowly to herself. Most of the information was known to her already.

"Pentacle: a magic star with five branches said to be the Star of David. Also the flaming star, which is called Agrippa's pentagram (was used in Magic)."

She frowned.

"Agrippa's pentagram?"

The name rang bells. She returned to the index and looked up Agrippa.

"Agrippa de Nettesheim 1486-1533. A man fascinated by the Cabala and magic which allows communication with the forces of a higher plane."

Suzie-Q looked across at the facing page. In the corner was a drawing of a strange creature, like a great horned goat but with the body of a human. In the centre of its head sat the five pointed star. Beneath this and to the left of the picture was a caption: *Baphomet, the composite idol said to have been worshipped by the Knights Templar*.

"Knights Templar. When we went to Cambridge, the Round Church in Bridge Street ... Templar sites ... round churches, that's it, they worshipped in these places, didn't they ... Oh ... Oh!"

She pulled down the *AA Book of the Road*. There was a fold-out map of southern England. She tore out the page and leapt across to the bed where the Merlin sheet was.

She pulled off the top of a felt tip pen, which lay on the floor, and hurriedly copied the red marks of the Merlin head office sites on to the AA map.

Cambridge, Aylesbury, Petersfield, Hastings and Agrippa Island. A point on the River Blackwater. Finally, there was London, smack in the centre.

"Smack in the centre ...

"Merlin's Mega head office, where Mr Le Mara sits, surrounded by it all."

Once she had made her mind up that her hunch was correct, it was an easy drawing to make.

She drew a circle connecting the five towns which surrounded London. Then there was the simple matter of connecting it all up.

Suzie-Q uncrumpled the National Theatre poster which she had ripped off the burger cafe window.

It came as no surprise.

She twisted the edge of the bedsheets into a tight knot.

The pentacles matched.

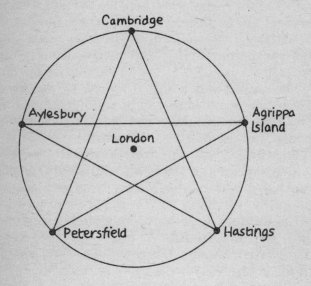

"... it was a dark choir ..."

Dizzy had fallen asleep, curled up into an awkward heap beside the hi-fi equipment. Very little remained of the compact disc player and the sticky patch had dissolved away into a fine, coloured powder.

The Battersea dawn was beginning to ease its way through the slits in the Venetian blinds. Lights still burned inside the shop. The SP25 Mark II continued to revolve but the autochanger had replaced the tone arm to its rest hours ago.

There was a sudden clunk as the shop bell sprang to life.

Sparks burst in, slamming the door behind him. He looked down at the waking Dizzy, and noticed the CD player.

"Slow blow fuse no good then?"

He peered more closely at the player's chassis.

145

"Bloody hell! Have you been having some wild party or what? I've done your tape, mate. Sorry it took all night. I don't know what's on this thing but it didn't want me to listen to it. Right little horror it was."

Dizzy blinked as one hand searched the floor for his glasses. Sparks continued as he began to examine the rear of the amplifier.

"Told yer you needed another amp, this thing's had it, Diz. It might be able to struggle with the cassette ... hey, what HAVE you been doing with all this stuff? I've never seen such bad burn-out on a piece of gear."

"It's been to the devil and back," said Dizzy with a hint of the melodramatic.

"Looks like it. Touch of the old Alice Coopers, eh? Anyway, like I said, we had a recording session at the studio, that delayed me for a start, and then this creep of a thing wouldn't play. Kept throwing up ERROR all the time."

Dizzy nodded.

"No problem though, not to Sparks. I bodged it a bit but it worked. Just meant I couldn't get to hear the disc myself. Pity, 'cos I was curious. It was really clever of me, stroke of genius, you might say. You see, compact disc players are record decks that go faster, a low-powered gas laser replaces the record stylus. That's what picks up the pits in the disc, samples, takes little pockets of the stuff ... "

"A laser? Did you say samples?" Dizzy said.

"Yeah, come on, Diz, you ain't that out of time. CDs work from laser beams. What I did was to record the thing back to front,

I tricked it, cut out the ERROR signal and it worked. Like a dream. The next thing was to get it into the phaser. No problem. We cut off all the top, boosted what I suppose was this choral line you mentioned and then ran it backwards again on to this cassette. It won't be perfect. I'd have liked to fine-tune the thing, but you wanted it here a bit sharpish, didn't you?"

He held up a plastic case containing a black cassette tape.

"Sliced like a peach. A real cross-section. One half of a compact disc."

Sparks looked suitably smug.

"It wasn't easy," he added.

"What is digital technique exactly?" asked Dizzy quietly. "I mean, I know roughly, but how does it all actually operate?"

Sparks crouched down by the amplifier again, tutting through his teeth as he redirected the cassette deck's lead into the amplifier.

"My little black box seems OK, but this compact disc player is bye byes. Was it struck by lightning? What did you say, digital eh? Well, put into your lingo, that means simple I suppose, a digit is a number, right? Like 1 2 3. A digital computer, for example, is one which works by a binary code. You know, the combo of 0 1 2 and so on? A switch which is on or off, it operates through a circuit conducting or not conducting and . . ."

"Hang on!" said Dizzy, "I want it really simple."

Sparks raised his eyes to the ceiling.

"It's a way of processing information. In sections, in bits. Yeah, that's it, in bits. Lots of things are digitally operated these days. It's fast, you see. Telephones, computers, watches, rockets, yeah, even missiles! Bombs!"

"Bombs?"

Dizzy flinched.

"What does it look like?"

"Look like?"

"Yes. Digital. If you had to describe it . . . "

Sparks laughed.

"It doesn't *look* like anything. But if you want some easy example then I suppose little pockets of information, sections of data, something like that."

Dizzy held his breath.

"And what is analogue then?"

Sparks pointed at the Jerry Lennox golden disc.

"That. A continuous signal. Straight down the middle! Like Jerry Lennox!"

"Could something . . . could something *hide*, be concealed inside digital information?"

Sparks slapped the side of his leg.

"Diz, my man, you just crease me. What on earth would want to hide inside digital processing? Here, the deck's fixed up. Simply slot your cassette in there and off you go. I'll catch you later. I want to know what this is all about and what it is that I've gone and creamed off for you."

Sparks looked at his watch.

"I might catch breakfast if Pollyanna's is open yet."

"But could something *hide*, be concealed in . . . ?"

"Yeah. I suppose so," said Sparks. "I'm hungry."

He was gone.

Dizzy lifted the Jerry Lennox single off the turntable.

Dizzy checked that all the connections were tight and then lowered the volume. Sparks had left everything ready for the tape to be played. The amplifier selector had been switched over and he had even swept the floor. He made sure that the front door was still unlocked. Even though it was only a recording of the compact disc, he had had more than his fill of odd events and he might need to do a runner.

He pressed the PLAY control on the tape deck and stood well back.

The speakers hummed.

A squawl of noise was somewhere there on the tape. It echoed in the background, threatening to cut into the fore. After a moment, the track began. The voices were distinct, and unmusical. Suzie-Q's description had been correct. It *was* like a choir. But it was a choir unlike any he had ever heard before.

At first there were only low moaning sounds, and a distant thud which sounded like the beat of a drum repeating a constant rhythm, over and over. Only a few voices could be detected clearly at first, but slowly the bolero grew.

The voices were insistent.

And grim.

149

If choir was the right description, it was a dark choir.

Dizzy struggled to understand the words, but they were sung in an unfamiliar language. It was an old language, he identified that much from his studying days.

After a moment a single word began to feature prominently amongst the garbled mixture. He listened carefully, straining his ears to hear it. Feeling braver, he crossed over to the amplifier and turned up the control.

The words hit him like a hammer.

"Divina. Gorgonus ex inferno. Baphomet!"

"That's some kind of Latin," he said. "It's weird Latin, though! DigiWave be blowed, that's something else!"

He had heard this name somewhere before. They spoke the name of an Ancient Demon.

The chanting rose to a point, like a wave, only to crash again. Dizzy looked down at his feet; they had been tapping out a beat in time with the chant and he hadn't noticed. Suddenly his entire body lurched forward with the tempo. It possessed power and he was shaking with the madness of it.

The room swayed around him.

There was an inner yielding, a wish to belong.

He pirouetted like a top, arms outstretched, open and wide, allowing the cries to fill his entire being.

"Baphomet. Baphomet. Baphomet."

Round and round he went, like the SP25.

He cried out, a wail of surrender.

"Master! Here I am!"

He felt his blood begin to boil, his heartbeat quickened, there was a pressure behind his eyes.

It pushed. Harder and harder and harder. He felt as though he was about to explode. Something dark crouched near, he caught sight of black folds from out of the corner of his eye. The room telescoped outwards.

The tape clicked off.

He fell back, stumbling against the browser racks.

Suzie-Q stood before the tape deck. Her finger still firmly held the OFF key down. The front door of the shop was open wide.

"Dizzy!" she ran to him. "Dizzy! What's happening?"

Dizzy Richards' breath came in short sharp intakes of pain. His cheeks were wet with tears and his chest burned. His eyes rolled in his head. He had lost control so easily, but he had listened to it undiluted. Uncluttered by electronic sounds. Sparks had done his job too well.

Suzie-Q held him tightly in her arms as he cradled her head in his hands.

"Suze," he spoke in a hushed, tired voice, "there's something we have to do."

She turned her head towards him. He looked old.

"It's going to be dangerous," he added. "Very dangerous."

"... Mr Le Mara would like you to join him ..."

Nick felt as though he had been stuffed inside an upright drainpipe. It was the strangest room he had ever been in. By pulling his knees up to his chin he found that he was able to crouch down and get a brief nap, but sleep hadn't come easily.

Although there were no windows, the sky peeped down into the tube from way above as if he were at the bottom of some kind of shaft. He guessed that it was a vent trap for the air conditioning – but at the moment it was simply a prison. After the door closed, there had been only the silence and the drift of the moon overhead to watch.

He had also observed the passing of a day: the creeping of the dawn, and the dusk, and now the approach of another evening. Moonrise would be upon him at any moment. He wondered how long he would have to remain there.

152

Perhaps he was destined to stay there for ever. No food, no drink, no sounds and no way out.

There was a shuffling outside.

The door swung open. The outline of a figure stood over him. He shadowed his eyes with a hand. The sudden intrusion of light made it difficult to see.

"Mr Le Mara would like you to join him," said a voice.

The door gaped even wider and he was roughly dragged up from his crouching position.

The corridor outside was dimly lit, but after spending so much time in a drainpipe room, Nick was not only finding it difficult to see anything, but also to stand. His legs and arms tingled and ached with a dull numbing pain.

He was pulled through the door and out into the corridor.

"Come on, we haven't got all day," said the voice.

There were two Guardians. It was impossible to tell whether or not they were the same men that had discovered him. They all looked so similar, bearing the usual anonymity which came with dark blue uniforms. Nick was too preoccupied with trying to discover whether or not there were tell-tale signs of scar tissue anywhere to bother.

He was still unsure about what he was dealing with, but over the past forty-eight hours he had begun to remember chunks of detail of the night with the Dark Side CD. Flashbacks. Moments of insight. They turned a corner and climbed a short staircase which led to a mezzanine floor.

Another short corridor led off from here. It all began to look familiar. They were returning to the round room.

Within moments the group stood before the entrance, the Guardians held his arms, squashed closely together on either side of him. One of the men leant forward and opened the door.

"Do come in," said a soft, polite voice.

One of the Guardians pushed him forward.

The place had changed.

Nick gawped at it all. It was now set out like something from a science fiction movie, but with strange dark medieval touches scattered here and there.

There was a heavy, sickly smell of incense. Shadowy purple wisps of smoke tangled their way across the room.

A white circle with a five-pointed star had been redrawn in thick white paint in the centre of the floor. At the points of the star were tall black candles on gleaming golden candlesticks.

In the centre stood an iron brazier upon which sat a round brass pot. The pot was in a direct line with the central opening in the domed roof. The flames of a small contained fire licked out from beneath.

The walls were daubed with fresh signs and symbols – geometric shapes drawn in chalk and an ochre-coloured paint, similar to the designs in the rest of the building.

The whole thing looked ridiculous to Nick. It was the incongruity of it all.

Against this semi-alchemist's setting was an

entire block of hi-tech equipment. To the left of the door stood a twenty-set-high bank of television monitors. They arched round the curve of the room, a row of at least thirty. Bright coloured screens showed the frame of a TV test card with the logo Lasers lit within the centre.

Above this was a digitally lit panel, displaying five names. Red indicator lights glowed beside each:

Cambridge – Round Church.
Aylesbury – The Abbey.
Petersfield – St Julian's.
Hastings – The Catacombs.
Agrippa Island – The Shrine.

Across the room, set on a rostrum about a foot above the floor, was a large polished desk. A hunched figure sat behind this desk in a deep comfortable-looking bucket seat which was turned away from Nick's view. Within the semi-darkness it was difficult to see who it was at first, but Nick could guess.

The man was looking out through one of the portico windows, surveying the evening lights of London.

"Good evening, young man. How fortuitous that you should join us. Le Mara's the name."

The chair swung round slowly.

"Simon Le Mara."

Light from the TV monitors caught the gem stones on his fist of rings. The dancing kaleidoscope of colour which was swept across the room dazzled Nick.

Nick peered into the gloom. He was adjusting to the light now, and it was getting easier to

155

see. Le Mara looked very like the occasional photograph which had appeared in the magazines. Thin-faced, his hair was swept back from his forehead in a deep widow's peak. The identity clincher came from the famous pointed goatee beard, joined by the thin moustache line which swept down on either side of his mouth. He was smartly dressed in a double-breasted suit with a tie, held in place by a silver pin, containing another even larger jewel.

"Welcome, we can watch the opening night of my new club together. I gather you've already got a membership card."

Nick looked for a way out, but there was none. There were six Guardians in the room with Le Mara. The two that had brought Nick stood sentry-like on either side of the doorway. Another two were busy adjusting the bank of monitors, and two more looked preoccupied with a large silver console positioned next to Le Mara's desk. The words MERLIN DIGITAL PROCESSOR were stamped on the side. Wires trailed out from the machine to the monitors, others disappeared out of one of the portico windows and then continued on in an upward direction towards the roof.

They were obviously waiting for something.

"This is all rather clever, you know," said Le Mara. "In a few hours' time the Incubi, that wonderful new DigiWave band, will perform at my new club. All that fresh young strength and talent and vitality dancing and having a good time to the sounds of DigiWave. It will all be mine and my partner's. My familiars will beam

156

all that concentrated energy over to the Merlin Megastore mast which is sitting above us."

"Familiars?" said Nick. He remembered something about witches and witches' cats. Demons disguised as animals.

Le Mara pointed upwards to the opening in the dome. A single slender finger traced a line downwards to the flame-caressed brazier set in the centre of the star.

"The signal will bring forth the Dark Lord, sacrifice will be made simultaneously at the five equal points from the central source of power. In the five Holy Places of the Order of the Templars, an ancient order, with ancient power. They were the obvious model for that which I needed."

His eyes sparkled as he adjusted his tiepin. His other hand pointed at the board.

"Merlin will have the greatest, most powerful source of hard rock in the world, all those musicians, and it will be HIS. My debt will be paid."

"His?" asked Nick.

"Baphomet, boy. Baphomet," whispered Le Mara.

One of the Guardians moved across from the door and stood beside Nick. He stretched out his hand in front of him.

There was the sound of something tearing, crackling, and then a sound like the crumpling of stiff paper. Nick watched in disbelief. The tips of the Guardian's fingers began to bulge, then the fingers themselves lengthened as cracks appeared below the quick of the fingernails.

Then they burst through the flesh.

Long, pointed talons.

Simon Le Mara laughed.

The Guardian reached up below his cap and removed the dark glasses. Coal fire burned within dark craters.

"My assistants, given me by the Dark Lord to help complete our task."

"But why . . . why . . . ?" Nick could hardly get his words out.

Le Mara stood up. His face became stern and angry as his voice toughened.

"Why? Why do you think, boy? Merlin is the largest pop industry in the world. A phoenix born out of the ashes of Dan Fauster's Upfront. I couldn't let Upfront die. I had plans, I could have the world, the potential was, is, there! Mindless stupid youth is so easily led and there's nothing – nothing as vital as the raw energy of the street. The street is where it is: pop music! Mega-business hype! Keep the people happy! Give them buns and circuses. They'll love it all, bless them! Give them DigiWave. Why not?"

The monitors began to flicker, the inside of a dazzling brightly lit room, like a dance floor, flashed on to the screens. People were busily rushing around preparing for something.

"What happened with Upfront made good business sense," continued Le Mara. "I became partners with a long-established businessman, that was all. He's always been a *very* good businessman."

The Guardian smiled.

"You're Dan Fauster," said Nick.

Le Mara clapped his hands in mock applause, and then threw back his head and laughed.

"Of course, you stupid little boy, that is, I was." His eyes sparkled. "I think I'd like you to meet my partner personally."

He shot a glance across to the Guardians before continuing.

"My partner's a little old-fashioned, though. He's been around a long time, you understand. He would appreciate some small sacrifice carried out in the traditional way; that's why we've kept you. You saved us the trouble of plucking someone from a grotty slot-machine arcade. Plenty of young souls there, you know. You're a little bonus, so to speak. Digital is clean but the old ways are so much better sometimes. And just think," he broke off with a snigger, "we won't have to put up with all those feathers."

Nick felt faint.

The laughter of the room echoed up into the dome above.

"... I'm good enough ..."

Suzie-Q felt as if she had been packed into a conference centre for zombies. It had to be her, they'd never have let Dizzy in. The queues outside had circled the Dean Street block many times. It was terrifying. All those kids with vacant expressions, simply standing in line like herded cattle, hardly saying a word. When there was speech it was repetitious. One girl who had stood behind her kept repeating the same phrase:

"I'm good enough, I'm good enough, I'm good enough."

Their minds were not their own any more. For weeks they had hidden in their rooms playing DigiWave over and over, wanting more and more. The opening night would be the realization of their dreams: a live performance. There were more of these kids than Suzie-Q had dared imagine. Some members of the crowd had

160

simply listened once and got their tickets. They were still "together", but one could see a look of anxious curiosity set hard within their open pupils.

Now she was in.

Squeezed like a sardine into a tight and heaving mass of flesh.

For the first few hours there had been a lot of the usual pop music played through gigantic horn-driven loudspeakers.

A strange green fizzy cocktail was being handed round by white-uniformed waiters. Oval trays were pushed into people's faces.

A pair of the waiters stood near Suzie-Q. They were busy collecting further glasses from a long table. Suzie-Q watched their backs. One of them looked awfully familiar. It was the plaits.

They turned round. Dead faces looked straight through her.

"Oh my God," she hesitated, wondering whether to run to them. "Josh . . . and Terry . . . what have they done to you?"

But she knew Josh had already joined. Now, so had Terry.

The drinks made their eyes spin and widen until they could open up no more. Suzie-Q kept away from it. The crowd was slowly getting dopier. The electric buzz of excitement and anticipation was truly infectious, Suzie-Q had difficulty concentrating. It was so easy to allow oneself to drift away with the multitude.

There were few Merlin store staff, but there were many Guardians, all with inane grins, fixed-featured faces.

She stood on tiptoe, looking for emergency doors, just in case. Her nerve ends tingled and her arm ached from the weight of the heavily laden bag which she had been carrying.

Suzie-Q moved across the dance floor towards the green EXIT sign.

In line from the door, but in the centre of the floor, squatted a large Monitor Control Console, a fold-back with a vast array of knobs and switches with tape decks and CD chassis players. There was one silver coloured master CD player, much larger than the others. Dizzy had told her there probably would be. A long thick bundle of cables rose up from this into the console and then into the gantry of lighting above. A spatter of lasers began to trace their multi-coloured grids across the heads of the crowd.

There were semi-doped cheers.

"Hi there, kids! Well, whatta you know! YOU WERE ALL GOOD ENOUGH!"

The announcement thundered down from the secret ceiling above.

The cheers and applause returned.

A peak-capped head bobbed up from the middle of the Control Console. The hands hovered above the controls.

The invisible host's voice quietened the crowd.

"Husshhhh. Now then, we're only seconds away from the Dark Hour, the Black Hour of Midnight, brace yourselves. TO BE AMONGST YOU VERY SOON, THE MERLIN MEGASTORE

CORPORATION IN ASSOCIATION WITH TEMPLAR INDUSTRIES PROUDLY PRESENT THE FIRST LIVE PERFORMANCE OF THE NEW SOUND. LET'S HEAR IT TOGETHER. LET'S ALL COUNT DOWN:

   Nine

   Eight

   Seven

Suzie-Q's hand gripped her bag.

   Six

   Five

   Four

Suzie-Q held her breath.

   Three

   Two

   One . . .

   BOYS AND GIRLS, IT'S DIGIWAVE AND . . . THE INCUBI!"

The audience heaved with the reverie of a Witches' Sabbat.

"... singing its heart out, with a purity of soul ..."

Simon Le Mara directed the operations from behind his desk like an agitated puppet master. Fingers clicked in this direction, and then that. Brief beckoning gestures told the Guardians to pan in on one part of the Lasers club floor or the other.

The round room was gorged with energy. The bank of TV monitors switched from presenting one huge composite screen to smaller sections, showing the activities at Lasers from a multitude of differing points of view.

Lights flashed a signal to Le Mara from the five Merlin headquarters. Fires would be lit and words would be sung at the equidistant points at precisely the right time.

Nick was too wound up with everything around him to feel sensibly scared. The Guardians had him tightly trussed up into a ball with white and silver cord. He was placed in a squatting position before the brazier around which deep blue flames now grew. A highly ornamented sword had been placed beside his feet, the Grand Master's. Le Mara said that it had belonged to the greatest of all Knights of the Ancient Order of the Templars, Jacques de Molay. Nick didn't care who it belonged to.

His eyes held the central cluster of monitors. A voice had announced the appearance of the Incubi, the crowd had cheered, but nobody had appeared yet.

"Check camera area 5," said Le Mara suddenly.

A light blinked simultaneously on a square of four monitors. A wild-faced, ginger-headed boy was swaying as though in a trance. The picture zoomed into focus for Le Mara's attention.

"Increase volume," commanded Le Mara.

The boy was humming the Templar mantra, the vocal from the Dark Side CD.

Le Mara smiled a smile of satisfaction.

"Security won't be a problem," he said. "They're all ours already."

A faraway thunderclap shook the club dance floor.

The monitors switched to a single large screen.

A piercing guitar note hovered in the air for a moment. There was the beat of a thousand drums, a grating, stomach-churning crunch of chords which sawed through the air above the audience. This time the ground visibly shook. The kids scuttled to the edges of the room, there

165

were shouts and cries as they all looked towards the central console.

DigiWave was coming.

The Control Console glowed, a brightening silver sheen.

The drawers of the bank of CD players slid tightly shut. The sampling was about to take place again, energised through the console and down into the master player.

The Guardian who stood within the centre removed his peaked cap, and then the dark glasses.

Fire eyes scanned the crowd. The head grew like an inflating balloon. The features stretched grotesquely. His mouth opened.

Hell came out.

He was the opener of the way.

The channel for Baphomet.

A long lapping silver tongue flowed out from between the teeth and blackening lips, lengthening and widening, twisting and wriggling in the air like an emerging snake. It grew and grew, moving upwards towards the ceiling and interweaving with the beam of the lasers.

Then the skin was shed.

There was wrinkling at first as a layer peeled slowly back, and then the flesh fell apart completely as though in accelerated decay. A pillar of solid light remained, shining like pure silver, a liquid stream of solid digital energy with a silver whip which flew around the room like a searching whirlwind.

The laser tongue searched the corners of the dance floor, sucking in the energy of the kids who swayed together in groups around the walls.

The master CD drawer slid open and the air became filled with silver bubbles, blown from somewhere within the player. They flowed outwards and upwards. Dozens upon dozens. An army of floating orbs which carried the creatures within. Crouched and waiting with itchy claws, needle teeth and hot eyes.

The Incubi. But hardly a rock band.

Above them, the laser lights connected across the room, casting a dazzling net of finely honed power.

Then the voices came.

Nick had heard them before. A chant, a contagious pulse, an ancient spell.

The Guardians at Lasers had frozen into stiff attitudes, unable to move. Metamorphosis began. The lower parts of their faces had dissolved away, the digital cries and chants burst from another, darker place. They had become a direct line to the old gods.

Back within the round room, Nick cried out. There was a force, a strong irresistible urge from within to join them. He screwed his face up as he fought the voice inside his head.

"Join us, join us."

A silvery blue fork of lightning shot down from the opening in the dome. The connection had been made.

Lasers was transmitting.

"Baphomet!" cried Le Mara in ecstasy.

Nick tried to throw himself back. The fork

remained, twisting and crackling from the ceiling to the floor.

DigiWave filled the air, the smoke from the incense combined with the weave of notes congealing into thickening globules, falling like muddy rain into splattering pools of liquid sound.

Nick's attention flicked back to the screen. Something which shone like a blue aura was being ripped from out of the kids by the silver tongue and taken into the laser pillar of power.

It was taking their souls. Thick wedges of life, draining away.

The orbs began their descent to the club floor, the bubble-like skin melting upon contact.

There was a rush of air from above.

Nick looked up and watched in amazement at what now appeared before him.

The precious vitality which was being collected at Lasers was now being spat down the lightning shaft from the roof, and into the sacrificial pot.

"Baphomet, my lord, are you well pleased?" whispered Le Mara.

"It's just technique, baby!"

Nick's head twisted sharply round to the bank of the monitor screens.

Le Mara stood up suddenly, throwing his chair backwards.

"What . . . what is that?" he boiled.

Nick looked hard at the screen.

"By the Control Console, close up, quickly," yelled Le Mara.

A group of six monitors homed in on the silver

island of light. There was a figure crouching there. At first Nick took it to be one of the incubi. But it wasn't. It was a small, round-faced, blonde kid with some kind of electrical equipment which she was connecting to the Console's control panel.

"Blow up the picture! Blow up!" screamed Le Mara.

" . . . **The way I do it, baby . . .** "

The lyrics smashed through the air, cutting and darting, weaving and fencing their way around the lascivious tongue of DigiWave.

The total monitor bank homed in on the figure.

"Suzie-Q!" cried Nick. "It's Suzie-Q!"

"Suzie-Q? Who or what is Suzie-Q? What's she got there?"

Le Mara had crossed the rostrum. He now stood at the edge of the pentacle. The lightning fork continued to twist angrily.

A bleached, skull-white head began to emerge from the top of the brazier pot. He was coming.

A heaving crumple of skin and bone struggled to rise.

"I don't believe it!" shouted Nick, his attention captured by the monitor screens. The voice in his head was a garbled whisper now. He hadn't noticed the pot as he struggled excitedly, pulling and tugging at the cords which held his arms and legs.

"It's Dizzy's record deck and she's plugged it straight into your machine! She's even got a record on it! What's she doing?"

"A record deck. Father of darkness! Analogue . . . ! No, no no!"

The monitors zoomed in on the record.

It was as bright as the sun as it travelled round at 45 revolutions per minute.

"Gold is light," screamed Le Mara. "It's the right path, get that damn thing off!"

Nick wondered what he meant. And then he realized.

" . . . **My art and craft, baby,**
It's just technique . . . !"

Jerry Lennox's original golden single was on the player, the one from the Bakelite frame in Dizzy's shop.

Gold – the metal of the Three Kings.

It was sending its straight analogue path into the heart of dark, crooked digital technology. It had been easy for Suzie-Q to fix it up. The kids were elsewhere in states of dark ecstasy and there had been that vital few minutes when the Guardians had undergone their change and been unable to move, frozen like moths in a chrysalis.

There was a crunch of hoof and bubble of skin within the pot at the centre of the circle.

"We've got to stop her . . . " Le Mara stepped forward, down off the rostrum, not looking where he was going.

The lightning crackled around his feet.

Like a suddenly yanked rug the fork swept across him and pulled him into the centre of the star.

The cry was long and terrible.

A golden shaft of sunlight rippled down from the roof of the dome, transmitted directly, courtesy of Lasers. It filled the room with its

170

warm rays. From within the beam a shimmering spectre, Fender Stratocaster guitar and long blonde curls, was singing and playing its heart out with a purity of soul.

A dark thing with wet black fur hanging from grey bones began to crawl from out of the brazier pot.

It roared, the goat-like horns twisted like the branches of a knotted bough. It was about to claim, when the shaft of light encircled its body.

The golden rays cocooned the form, forcing it back. The creature would have to return.

But there was also a debt to settle.

With the partner.

Le Mara screamed and screamed again.

A claw grabbed his leg and heaved, pulling him into the creature's embrace. The heavy folds of greying decay sucked him in and down. Back into the darkness.

Nick rolled to one side and tugged hard at his bonds.

With a sudden twist and snap at the cord he was free.

He hunted for the door. The Guardians, only half transformed, were frozen where they stood. As the rays had touched them so their skin had tightened, forcing out the remainder of what lurked within into the light.

The dome above shook. A fissure broke across, plaster and brick began to crumble and fall into the centre of the pentacle.

Nick headed for the door.

Where now? Ventilation system! The lift shaft,

the air ducts, if he was lucky they would deliver him down through the building.

At the end of the corridor he found the stairs to the next set of lift doors.

He threw the catches on the service panel and opened the door.

With a gulp, he leapt into the chute and began his descent.

The three of them had watched together, from the cover of Tottenham Court Road Underground station as the fire engines, ambulances and police had gathered at the entrance of the Merlin Megastore.

The top of the building had been swept clean away. A freak weather condition, one fireman had said, something like a mini tornado.

Suzie-Q held Nick tightly, almost crushing him. She wouldn't let him go. Dizzy's arms enveloped them both. There would be little point in saying anything. Who would believe them?

The kids who had emptied out from the club on to the street didn't seem to know what they were doing there. Josh and Terry were leaning against a shop window, wondering why they were dressed up like ship's stewards. The fireman had told Dizzy that the kids would be OK. It was probably because of all the fumes. Either that or spiked drinks.

The police thought there could be a connection with the Oxford Street fire, but they weren't saying anything yet . . .

"Pity about that dome," the fireman said,

"totally destroyed, the entire floor. Struck by lightning, they think. Who'd have thought it, in Oxford Street?"

Suzie-Q held out the Jerry Lennox disc for Dizzy to take.

Dizzy shook his head.

"Keep it. It's yours." He winked. "It's always belonged to you. I'm proud of you. Your father would be proud of you too."

Suzie-Q wrinkled her nose, "But we don't know who . . . "

She trailed off.

"See you kids later, perhaps you've found the sound for this new band," said Dizzy as he turned to walk down Charing Cross Road. "DigiWave, maybe?"

He walked away, whistling an old Lovin' Spoonful song.

What a day for a daydream,
What a day for a day-dreaming boy!"

The dawn began to creep across the sky.

"What time is it?" asked the fireman.

Suzie-Q didn't hear the question. Nick had fallen asleep. He had a lot of catching up to do.

"I think you kids ought to get along home. Just let the ambulance crew check you over first."

A nurse by the roadside beckoned to Terry and Josh.

The fireman stopped and looked into the window of a large electronics shop. A whole new range of cheap digital watches and computer equipment had been announced. A new line from the Merlin Megastore, said the white card stuck against the glass.

The fireman pressed his nose against the window.

"Gotta get a watch," he said.

As he turned away, the spots of LED light on the digital watch faces narrowed into sharp tiny points of redness.

The glowing eye of the digital computer disc drive narrowed into slit green and watched from the shelf above as he crossed the road.